Buried Treasure!

Jessica and Ellen carried the metal box up to Ellen's bedroom and locked the door. Ellen pursed her lips, sawing the rusty box lock with her father's hacksaw.

"It's almost . . . there!" The lock fell on the floor.

"Shhh," said Jessica. She wasn't sure if she'd heard someone.

Ellen peered out into the hall. "All clear," she said.

"Good," said Jessica. She opened the lid and blew away a layer of dust and dirt.

"Omigod!" whispered Ellen. Inside was a large pile of yellowed twenty-dollar bills, still in their wrappers. Underneath were two old-fashioned photographs and some faded letters.

Jessica snatched the money off the pile and began counting.

"How much? How much?" asked Ellen.

"Two . . . two hundred dollars!" Jessica couldn't believe their luck. "We're rich!"

Bantam Books in the SWEET VALLEY TWINS series
Ask your bookseller for the books you have missed

SWEET VALLEY TWINS

Buried Treasure

Written by
Jamie Suzanne

Created by
FRANCINE PASCAL

A BANTAM BOOK®

TORONTO · NEW YORK · LONDON · SYDNEY · AUCKLAND

RL 4, 008–012

BURIED TREASURE
A Bantam Book/March 1988

Sweet Valley High is a registered trademark of Francine Pascal.

Sweet Valley Twins is a trademark of Francine Pascal.

Conceived by Francine Pascal.

Produced by Cloverdale Press Inc.,
133 Fifth Avenue, New York, N.Y. 10003

Cover art by James Mathewuse.

ISBN 0-553-15533-4

Published simultaneously in the United States and Canada

Bantam Books are published by Bantam Books, Inc. Its
trademark, consisting of the words "Bantam Books" and
the portrayal of a rooster, is Registered in U.S. Patent and
Trademark Office and in other countries. Marca Regis-
trada. Bantam Books, Inc., 666 Fifth Avenue, New York,
New York 10103.

Printed and bound in Great Britain by
Cox & Wyman Ltd., Reading

To Page McBrier

One

Jessica Wakefield looked at the small, unopened metal box and shook her head in disbelief. The last place she ever thought she'd discover buried treasure was in Ellen Riteman's backyard.

It had been a cloudless Saturday afternoon in Sweet Valley. Jessica and Ellen were in the living room of Ellen's house watching a music video. Ellen's little brother Mark appeared in the doorway with tears in his eyes. Whiskers, the Ritemans' cat, had attacked Mark's pet parakeet Leon, and Mark wanted to have a funeral for the bird. He'd convinced Ellen and Jessica to help bury him.

After locating a spot in the backyard under a tree, Mark started to dig. A few minutes later, the shovel hit something.

"I think I hit a root," he said.

"Let me try," Jessica said. "It feels like metal." She then scooped away some more dirt.

Mark peered down at the hole. "It's a box!" he said.

Jessica got down on her hands and knees, and she and Ellen scraped away the rest of the dirt by hand. Very carefully, they lifted a small, rusty metal box out of the hole. It was sealed with a sturdy lock.

"Wow!" said Mark. "It's buried treasure!"

Jessica and Ellen exchanged glances. "Back up, Mark," said Ellen. "Let me see."

As the girls stood staring at the box, Jessica knew that she and Ellen were thinking the very same thing. The last thing they wanted to do was share the contents of the box with Mark. Still, Jessica couldn't help feeling excited. A real buried treasure! She was dying to find out what was inside.

"I want to open it," said Mark. "We can wait to bury Leon." He eagerly tugged at the lock.

"Later," said Ellen. "Come on, Mark. We can't interrupt a *funeral*." As she pulled Mark back, he stumbled over Jessica's foot.

Jessica let out a scream. "Ow! Watch it," she said. "That's my bad ankle." Several weeks earlier she'd injured her ankle. Although she had completely recovered, she still worried about hurting it again.

"Sorry," mumbled Mark.

Jessica knelt down and rubbed her foot. Maybe this was just the distraction she and Ellen needed to get rid of Mark. She caught Ellen's eye and then moaned dramatically. "Ohhhh," she cried. "I think you hurt it again."

Mark shifted his weight and stared at the ground. "I didn't do it on purpose," he said.

Jessica stretched out her arms. "Help me into the house," she groaned. "I need to put my foot up."

"But what about the buried treasure?" said Mark. "And Leon?"

"Don't you have any manners, Mark?" said

Ellen. "You practically crippled Jessica, and all you're worried about is that stupid box." She bent down and wrapped Jessica's left arm around her shoulder. Mark stood very still. "The least you can do is help me," Ellen snapped. Mark quickly wedged himself under Jessica's right arm.

Ellen and Mark escorted Jessica into the house and helped her onto the living room sofa. "Now what?" said Mark.

Jessica fluttered her eyelids. "I think I'm going to need my crutches," she said. "They're somewhere in my closet. At home."

"But I hardly touched you," Mark said.

Jessica sat up and rubbed her foot. "The doctor told me to be extremely careful."

Ellen nodded in agreement. "Mark, since *you* hurt Jessica's ankle, *you* should go get her crutches."

Mark glanced at the backyard. "But what about—"

"Mark!" said Ellen. "If Jessica has to go back to the doctor, you're going to be in really big trouble."

Mark narrowed his eyes suspiciously. "OK," he said. "But you'd better not open that treasure until I get back."

"Don't worry about it," said Ellen. She and Jessica watched Mark rush out the front door and disappear down the street.

Jessica immediately hopped up and ran toward the back door. "Hurry," she said. "We don't have much time."

Several blocks away at the Wakefield house, Jessica's identical twin sister, Elizabeth, was sitting in her bedroom with her best friend, Amy Sutton. Although it was hard to tell Jessica and Elizabeth apart, the two girls couldn't have been more different. Jessica lived for the moment and was interested in clothes, movie stars, and boys. Elizabeth, who was four minutes older, preferred books to music videos. She liked to spend her spare time working on *The Sweet Valley Sixers*, the sixth-grade newspaper she'd helped start.

Elizabeth glanced over at Amy, who was sitting cross-legged on the floor, bent over a large sheet of poster board. "How about this?" said Amy. "Your Money's in Good Hands with Elizabeth. Vote E. W. for Student Council Treasurer."

Elizabeth shook her head. "No," she said. "Too flat." The two thought quietly for a moment. "Wake Up with Wakefield?" Elizabeth suggested.

"What's that have to do with being student council treasurer?" inquired Amy.

Elizabeth shrugged. "I was trying to come up with something catchy," she said.

"Don't worry," said Amy. "Anything's better than Don't Despair with Peter."

Elizabeth laughed. Peter DeHaven was her competition for student council treasurer, and even Elizabeth, who was usually kind to everyone, had to admit that Peter was a little odd.

Amy jumped up and hiked her pantlegs way above her ankles. "Ms. Wyler, I think you made a mistake on my math grade," she whined. "I should have gotten a ninety-eight, not a ninety-seven." She moved her eyebrows up and down like Peter.

Elizabeth couldn't stop laughing. "Amy, that's not nice," she said. Just then the doorbell rang.

"You'd better watch it," said Elizabeth. "That's probably Peter right now." She and Amy ran downstairs and opened the front door. It was Mark, Ellen Riteman's little brother.

"What's wrong?" asked Elizabeth.

Mark was out of breath. "Jessica needs her crutches," he said. "I accidentally bumped her ankle. It wasn't my fault."

"Her bad ankle?" said Elizabeth. "Oh, no!"

"Is she in pain?" said Amy.

"I'm not sure," said Mark. "I think she'll be OK. I hardly even touched it."

Elizabeth relaxed a little. Jessica *did* have a tendency to be a bit overdramatic. Maybe she was just playing it safe by using her crutches.

Mark stared anxiously upstairs. "Can I get the crutches now?"

Elizabeth led Mark to Jessica's room. "Good luck finding them," she said, opening the door. Jessica's room was in its usual condition. Clothes were flung everywhere, and several dirty dishes and a crumpled cookie carton littered the floor.

"Wow," said Mark. "I thought *my* room was bad."

"Let's try the closet first," Elizabeth said. She dug around for several minutes. "What's this?" she said. She pulled out a large cardboard box and peered inside. "I don't believe it." The box was filled with chocolate bars. "She hasn't sold a single one," she said.

The chocolate bars had been distributed to everyone in the sixth grade nearly a month earlier. They were supposed to be selling them to earn money for a class trip to Disneyland.

"How's she going to sell all those chocolate bars by next week?" said Amy. It was her job to collect the money every week and give it to Ms. Wyler, their homeroom teacher, for safekeeping.

"Beats me," said Elizabeth. She began rummaging through the closet again. "Hmm," she said finally, "they're definitely not in here."

Mark looked around the room. "How about under the bed?" he said. He ran over, pulled up the bedspread, and pushed several pairs of mismatched socks aside. He popped his head back out and grinned. "I found them," he said. He dragged the crutches out and quickly hurried down the stairs. " 'Bye," he called.

Elizabeth looked anxiously down the stairs. "Mark?" she said. Mark stopped. "Would you tell Jessica to call me?" she asked. Mark nodded. Elizabeth turned to Amy. "I hope she's OK."

As soon as Mark had left the Ritemans', Jessica and Ellen carried the metal box up to Ellen's bedroom and locked the door. Now they were both bent over the rusty lock. "Hurry up," Jessica was saying. "He'll be back soon."

Ellen pursed her lips and continued to saw at the lock with the hacksaw she'd found in her father's toolbox. "It's almost . . ." She tugged on the lock. "There!" The lock fell to the floor.

"Shh," said Jessica. She cocked her head and listened for a moment. She wasn't sure if she'd heard someone. "Check the door," she whispered.

Ellen peered out into the hall. "All clear," she said. She closed the door and locked it again.

"Good," said Jessica. Very carefully she opened the lid. She blew away a layer of dust and dirt.

"I can't believe it!" whispered Ellen. On the top of the chest were a large pile of yellowed twenty-dollar bills, still in their wrappers. Underneath were two old photographs and some faded letters.

Jessica snatched the money off the top of the pile and began counting.

"How much?" said Ellen.

Jessica couldn't believe their luck. "Two hundred dollars," she said. She tossed the money in the air. "We're rich!" she cried. She and Ellen began giggling and hopping all over the bedroom.

"We're rich," screamed Ellen. "Rich, rich, rich." She danced around some more and then ran back over to the box. "Let's see what else there is," she said. "Maybe we can find out where the money came from."

Trembling with excitement, the two girls removed the photographs and the letters. The photos were of a man and a woman. The woman was quite beautiful. She had dark hair and dark eyes and was seated in a carved wooden chair. Covering her shoulders was a silky-looking flowered shawl. Her dress draped gracefully to the floor. The portrait of the man was completely different. He had on coveralls and stood stiffly beside a tractor. His large hands clutched a garden rake.

"Let's open the letters," said Ellen.

Jessica removed the first one. It was written in neat old-fashioned script. The date on it was March 13, 1928. "Dearest Jane," it began. "Yes, I do remember the first time we met. You were about eight years old, I was nine. Your father had brought you along to meet the new gardener, and I was outside our cottage, playing with some old bricks. Your father helped you out of the car and introduced us. I thought you were the most beautiful girl I'd ever met. I still do." Jessica and Ellen sighed.

"How romantic," said Ellen. "Love letters."

Jessica read on. "Dearest, I know that your father has opposed our marriage and is pressuring you to marry the 'more suitable' young man he has chosen. Please, Jane, I beg you to reconsider. What could be greater than our love?"

Jessica folded the letter. "Is that it?" said Ellen.

Jessica picked up the next letter. "Maybe this one has her answer." She quickly skimmed the contents. "Uh-oh. Not good. He tells Jane that if she loves him, she should have the courage to stand up to her father. He's proud to be the gardener's son."

"I think she should marry the man she loves," said Ellen. "Don't you?"

Jessica nodded and read through another letter. "Wow," she said. "Now he's begging her to elope with him. The two hundred dollars is money he'd saved so they could run away."

"This is like a movie or something," said Ellen with a sigh.

"I know," said Jessica. She read the last letter and frowned. "Listen to this," she said. "Dearest Jane, I wish only to spend the rest of my life with you. Meet me tonight at six o'clock under the grape arbor. I won't ask again, my dear Jane. No matter what happens, I will always love you. William."

Ellen stared at the letters. "Is that the last one?" she said.

Jessica nodded sadly. "Poor William. What do you think happened? Did she marry him or not?"

"I think if she'd married him, she would've spent the money," said Ellen.

"Maybe," said Jessica. "Or maybe she was rich enough not to need his money." They both sat quietly for a moment, still wrapped up in the story.

Jessica picked up the two hundred dollars. "What do you think we should do with the money?" she asked.

"If we tell everyone what we found, then we have to share the money with Mark," said Ellen.

"Right," said Jessica.

"Or," said Ellen, "Mom would want me to find out who lived in this house before us and see if it's their money."

Jessica and Ellen stared at the pile of bills. They each knew what the other was thinking. Jessica cleared her throat. "We *could* just tell Mark that all we found were some love letters," said Jessica.

"That's true," said Ellen. "He doesn't have to know about the money. We'll just divide it. A hundred dollars apiece."

Jessica quickly split it up. "Swear you won't say a word to anyone."

Ellen put her hand on her heart. "I swear." She stuffed her share into her back pocket and unlocked the bedroom door. "Come on," she said. "Help me take this box back to the yard before Mark sees us."

* * *

When Mark hurried into the Ritemans' living room, he was relieved to see Jessica sitting right where he'd left her. "Here are your crutches," he said, thrusting them into her hand. "Elizabeth says you should call her."

"Thanks," said Jessica. She delicately hoisted herself off the couch. "She's probably worried, right?"

Mark nodded, then quickly looked around the living room. "Where's Ellen?"

"Out in the yard," Jessica said. "She's trying to get that rusty old lock off the chest."

Mark ran out the back door. He saw Ellen look up and wave at him. "Perfect timing," she said. "I just broke the lock."

Jessica hobbled over. "Oh, good. Let's see what's inside."

The girls opened the chest and riffled through the contents. "Hmm," Ellen said. "Just some old letters and photographs."

Mark pushed his sister aside. "Let me see," he said. He peered inside the chest.

"I guess it wasn't buried treasure after all," said Jessica.

Mark looked at Jessica and then at Ellen. "Are you sure you guys didn't open this while I was gone?" he asked suspiciously.

"Of course not," said Ellen. "What do you think we are?" She swung her gaze over to the tiny cardboard box still sitting on the lawn. "What about Leon?" she said. "Are we going to bury him or not?"

"I guess so," Mark muttered. He sighed and picked up the shovel. Even though everything looked perfectly normal, something still didn't seem right to Mark. He suspected that somehow he'd been tricked.

Two

◇

Elizabeth paced her bedroom floor nervously. What had happened to Jessica? Suppose she was on her way to the hospital or something? When she'd phoned Ellen Riteman's house, there had been no answer. Just then Elizabeth heard the front door slam.

"I'm home," called Jessica.

Elizabeth raced to the top of the stairs. "Jessica! Are you OK?"

Jessica looked up in surprise. "Of course. Why?" She suddenly remembered her ankle and that she'd forgotten to call Elizabeth. "Oh, Lizzie," she said, clapping her hand over her mouth. "I forgot, didn't I?"

"I've been so worried all afternoon," said Elizabeth.

Jessica threw down a pile of packages. "False alarm," she said apologetically. "I feel fine now."

"Thank goodness," said Elizabeth. She was so relieved that she sat down with a thud on the stairs.

Jessica stared at Elizabeth. "You really *were* worried, weren't you?" she said.

"Of course I was!" Elizabeth answered. "If I didn't hear from you in another five minutes, I was going to call Mom. Or maybe even the police. No one even knew where you were."

Jessica sat down beside Elizabeth and gave her a hug. "I'm really, really sorry, Lizzie," she said. "My ankle just felt so much better that Ellen and I decided to go to the mall."

Elizabeth smiled and shook her head. "So I noticed," she said, staring at the pile of packages. She playfully punched Jessica's arm. "I thought you didn't have any money."

"I don't," Jessica replied quickly. "These things belong to Ellen. I was just carrying them for her."

Elizabeth looked doubtfully at her sister. "I don't get it," she said. "Why did you bring them here?"

"You won't believe what happened today," Jessica said, changing the subject abruptly. She grabbed one of the bags and pulled out a brand-new Walkman. "I found this at the mall!"

"Jess!" exclaimed Elizabeth. "You actually *found* it? That's incredible." Several weeks earlier Jessica had carelessly left her own Walkman outside and it had been ruined in the rain. She'd been begging her parents for a new one ever since, but they weren't about to give her a second chance.

"It is incredible," Jessica said, shaking her head. "But it's true. It was sitting in this shopping bag on a bench outside Sweet Valley Fashions."

"You're so lucky," said Elizabeth. "It's exactly like the one you ruined too."

"I know," said Jessica. She stood up abruptly and began to gather the packages. "Thanks for worrying about me," she said. "I'm sorry I forgot."

"That's OK," Elizabeth replied with a grin. "I

should have known my goofy sister would forget completely about calling."

"The student council elections are just two weeks away. Who are you going to vote for as president?" Julie Porter asked Elizabeth in school on Monday. They were in their weekly cooking class, making mini-pizzas.

Elizabeth sprinkled flour on the dough and picked up a rolling pin. "That's easy," she said. "Olivia Davidson."

"Me too," said Julie.

Olivia was sure to win the election, Elizabeth thought. She didn't even know who Olivia was running against.

"Have you written your speech?" Julie asked.

"Not yet," said Elizabeth. "Amy's my campaign manager, so she wants to help with it."

"Aren't you nervous about giving a speech in front of the whole school?" said Julie. "I would be."

Elizabeth nodded. "I'm trying not to think about that part." She finished rolling out the dough. "Now what?"

Julie looked at the recipe. "We spread on the tomato sauce."

A commotion broke out on the other side of the room. "Gross!" someone shouted. The entire class rushed over to see what was going on. Peter De-Haven was staring sadly at his pizza. His partner, Charlie Cashman, pointed an accusing finger at him. "He's putting dead flies in there," he said.

"I am not!" shouted Peter.

Mrs. Gerhart, the cooking teacher, clucked her

tongue. "Shame on you both," she said. She clapped her hands loudly. "Everyone, please! Back to your cooking stations."

Elizabeth could hear a lot of snickering as she and Julie returned to their tomato sauce.

"I feel sorry for Peter," said Julie. "Everyone always picks on him."

"I know," said Elizabeth. She thought about how she and Amy had made fun of him the other day, and felt guilty. "He's not that bad, really," she added. "Just weird, that's all."

As soon as the bell rang, Elizabeth and Julie made their way down the hall to homeroom. Ms. Wyler's classroom was at the other end of Sweet Valley Middle School, and with only five minutes between classes, Elizabeth always felt as if she were rushing. She heard someone calling her name and turned. "Hi, Amy," she said.

"How's this?" said Amy. "Elizabeth Makes Cents. Get it? Cents, sense."

"That's cute," said Julie.

Amy beamed. "It came to me while I was doing my math homework."

"That makes *sense*," said Elizabeth with a grin.

All three girls groaned. They walked into the classroom just as the bell rang.

Ms. Wyler waited for everyone's attention. "Before we begin, is there any candy money this week?" she said.

Elizabeth was surprised to see Jessica raise her hand. As usual, Jessica was sitting on the other side of the room with Lila Fowler and Ellen Riteman. All three girls belonged to the exclusive Unicorn Club.

The Unicorns knew they were popular, and always acted like they were special.

Jessica waved a five-dollar bill. "Here, Ms. Wyler," she said.

Elizabeth frowned. She hadn't remembered Jessica going out to sell candy since Saturday.

Now Ellen Riteman was waving a five-dollar bill. "Might as well turn mine in also," Ellen said.

Ms. Wyler looked really pleased. "Good work," she told the class. She handed the money to Amy. "Please make sure this goes into my locker sometime today," she said.

Ms. Wyler opened her math book. "Class, let's turn to page fifty-nine."

As Ms. Wyler droned on, Elizabeth absent-mindedly scribbled on her notebook. ELIZABETH MAKES CENTS, she wrote. She smiled and then filled in the letters with red Magic Marker. Amy had come up with a great idea, she thought. It would be a perfect campaign slogan.

After school Amy came over to the Wakefields' to help make posters. "We'll put them up tomorrow," she said. "Maybe we can even get Ken to help." Ken Matthews was Amy's "sort-of" boyfriend. Amy carefully sprinkled a little red glitter across Elizabeth's name. "This'll help your name stand out," she said.

Elizabeth hesitated. It seemed so flashy to her. "Are you sure?" she asked.

"How else are people going to notice it?" Amy asked.

"I guess," said Elizabeth. She looked at the

small clock on the dresser. "It's six o'clock already. Can you stay for dinner?"

"Sure," said Amy. "Let me call my mom."

Elizabeth ran downstairs to ask her mother's permission. As she burst through the door, she said, "What smells so good?"

"Frozen pizza," her mother replied. Mrs. Wakefield worked part-time as an interior designer, and didn't always have time to cook.

"Oh, no," said Elizabeth.

"What's the matter?" her mother asked. "I thought you liked pizza."

Jessica wandered in from the living room, wearing Elizabeth's favorite pair of sweatpants. "We made pizza in cooking class today!" she said.

The twins' older brother, Steven, stuck his head in the door. "And *we* had pizza for lunch," he added. Steven was a freshman at Sweet Valley High.

Mrs. Wakefield sighed. "Maybe we should go to the Dairi Burger." The Dairi Burger was the popular hamburger stand where the high-schoolers hung out. Sometimes the Unicorns held their meetings there.

"Can Amy come?" asked Elizabeth.

"Fine with me," said Mrs. Wakefield. "Your father won't be home until late."

Mr. Wakefield was a successful lawyer in Sweet Valley. Sometimes his busy practice kept him at his office until late in the evening.

Ten minutes later Mrs. Wakefield pulled into the Dairi Burger with Elizabeth, Amy, Jessica, and Steven. Outside, a group of teenagers were sitting on a car hood, talking.

Steven immediately noticed several people he knew, and realized he didn't want to be seen with his mother. "I'll go in and order, Mom," he said. "We can eat in the car."

"I thought we'd eat inside," said Mrs. Wakefield. She opened the door and got out of the car.

Jessica could tell what Steven was thinking. "That's OK, Mom," she said. "Steven and I can go and bring the stuff back to the car."

Mrs. Wakefield headed for the door. "Don't be silly," she said, and walked purposefully into the Dairi Burger.

Jessica looked at Steven and shrugged. No point in making a big deal about it now.

Soon they were all sitting in a booth near the front. Steven ordered two Dairi-Deluxe burgers and two orders of fries. He finished everything in less than five minutes. "Charity?" he asked, reaching for Elizabeth's fries.

Elizabeth slapped his arm. "I'm not finished yet," she said.

He turned to Jessica, who put her hand protectively over her fries. "Don't be such a pig, Steven," she said.

"Steven," said Mrs. Wakefield, "if you chewed more slowly, you'd fill yourself up a little better."

Steven noisily slurped the last of his milk shake. "OK, OK," he said. "I'll try."

A group of people entered the restaurant. "Look," whispered Amy. "It's Peter DeHaven."

Elizabeth stared at Peter. There was definitely something a little strange about him. Maybe it was his clothes. Most of the time he wore the same pair of brown pants with a matching belt and sturdy oxford shoes. Tonight, though, there was something different about him.

Amy giggled. "Look at his pants."

Elizabeth leaned forward. Instead of the usual pants and belt, Peter had on a new pair of brightly colored surfer shorts. He looked pretty silly in them, especially since he still had on his brown socks and brown shoes. Most embarrassing of all, though, was the price tag that dangled from his back pocket.

Jessica looked at Elizabeth and Amy and rolled her eyes. Steven snorted into his milk shake container and tried not to laugh. Jessica began to snicker loudly.

Peter looked over at her and realized that all eyes were on him. He shifted his weight uncomfortably and stared glumly at the floor. One of the high school boys walked slowly past. As soon as he reached Peter, he tugged sharply on the price tag and then kept walking. Peter spun around angrily. "Hey!" he shouted. His hand groped across his back pocket and felt the tag. His face flushed crimson.

This was too much for Steven. He began to laugh so loudly that now people turned to stare at him.

Peter looked at Steven, horrified. Then, without another word, he ran outside.

"Real nice, Steven," Elizabeth said.

Steven made a face. "I couldn't help it," he said.

Jessica was still laughing. "Wait'll they hear about this at school."

"Poor Peter," said Amy.

Jessica and Steven howled. Mrs. Wakefield looked at them with disapproval.

Elizabeth shook her head. "You know, he's

really not that bad," she said. "If he'd do something with his hair and get someone to help him with his clothes, he'd almost be cute."

Jessica giggled. "A Peter DeHaven makeover," she said.

Steven moved Elizabeth's french fries closer to him. "Why should you care?" he said. "Do you have a crush on him?"

Elizabeth wrinkled her nose. "Gross." She snatched her plate of french fries back. "It was only a comment, Steven," she said. "Don't get the wrong idea."

"Jessica, will you hurry up?" Elizabeth called. "We're going to be late." It was the next morning, and Elizabeth stood at the bottom of the stairs and waited. If she hadn't needed Jessica's help carrying her campaign posters, she would have left already.

Jessica appeared at the head of the stairs. "How does this look?" she asked. Jessica was wearing a pair of pink stretch pants with a baggy, purple sweatshirt. Purple was the Unicorns' favorite color.

"Good," said Elizabeth. "Where'd you get the sweatshirt?"

"I traded with Lila," Jessica said. "You know that sweatshirt with the lion on it that I never wear?"

"That's *my* sweatshirt!" said Elizabeth. "I got it from Aunt Shirley for Christmas last year, remember?"

"But you never wear it," said Jessica. "You don't even like it. You said it's too bright."

"But that doesn't mean I said you could give it away," said Elizabeth.

"I'm sorry, Lizzie. I didn't think you'd care. Want me to get it back?"

Elizabeth laughed. "You're too much," she said. "I'm probably the only girl in Sweet Valley whose sister trades away her clothes."

"I'll talk to Lila this afternoon," said Jessica.

Elizabeth shook her head. "OK, but now let's just go," she cried.

Later, as Elizabeth hurried down the hall, she noticed that several people had already put their campaign posters up. Olivia Davidson's were beautiful. Olivia was an excellent artist, and she'd obviously done all the work herself.

Elizabeth spotted Peter DeHaven hanging a poster near the cafeteria. She decided to take a quick peek. "Hi, Peter," she said.

Peter jumped when he heard his name. "Oh, hi, Elizabeth," he said, turning around. He pointed to his poster. "What do you think?"

Elizabeth stared at his poster. *It looks boring,* she thought. It looked as though he'd scribbled his campaign motto on with pencil. She was glad Amy had talked her into using a little glitter. "Uh, it's nice," she said. She stared uncomfortably at the floor. "Peter! You got new shoes!"

Peter looked at his feet. "Yup."

Elizabeth had never seen him in a pair of sneakers. They looked a little strange with his brown socks. What if he asked her what she thought of *them*? "Gotta go," she blurted.

Elizabeth bolted down the hall toward English class. She made it to her seat just as the bell rang.

* * *

By lunchtime everyone in the sixth grade was talking about Peter's new sneakers. At the exclusive Unicorns' table Lila Fowler said, "Do you believe it? And with brown socks too. Barf-o."

"Peter's such a nerd," said Ellen. All the Unicorns laughed.

Jessica couldn't wait to tell everyone what had happened at the Dairi Burger. After the Unicorns heard the story, they all shrieked with laughter. "Jessica, that's hysterical," said Janet Howell. "I wish I'd been there." Janet was the eighth-grade president of the Unicorns, and her approval really mattered to Jessica.

"Thanks," Jessica replied modestly.

Janet clapped her hand over her mouth. "I just had the greatest idea," she said. "Listen." The Unicorns huddled close together. As Janet whispered, the others nodded in agreement. Janet finished whispering and straightened back up. "So we'll do it tomorrow, OK?" she said. The Unicorns nodded in unison. "OK," they chorused.

Jessica grinned and smiled to herself. This was the meanest trick they'd played in a long time. She couldn't wait.

Three

◇

Ms. Wyler looked around the class and frowned. "Amy, may I speak to you for a minute?" she said. As Amy got up from her chair, she leaned over and whispered to Elizabeth, "Ken says he'll help us with the posters after school."

"Great," said Elizabeth.

Ms. Wyler waited until Amy was beside her desk. "Amy," she said quietly, "did you remember to add yesterday's candy money to the amount in my locker?"

Amy clapped her hand over her mouth. "Sorry, Ms. Wyler," she said. "It's still in my desk. I'll get it."

Ms. Wyler put her hand on Amy's arm. "No, wait," she said. She lowered her voice. "I'm afraid the money for the class trip has disappeared."

Amy gasped. "But it was there last week," she said. "I took the key from your desk and put the money into the cigar box in your locker myself."

Ms. Wyler looked distressed. "And when I went to get something from my locker this morning, the cigar box was missing. I don't know what we're going to do. I've looked everywhere."

Amy felt terrible. She was supposed to be in

charge of that money, and now it was gone. What were people going to think?

Ms. Wyler got the class's attention. "I have some very bad news," she said. "It appears that someone has taken our candy money."

Everyone began talking at once. "You mean somebody stole it?" shouted Charlie Cashman.

"I'm afraid so," said Ms. Wyler. "The last time Amy or I remember seeing that cigar box was last week."

Amy stood uncomfortably next to Ms. Wyler's desk.

"But what about our trip to Disneyland?" asked Julie.

Ms. Wyler sighed. "Unless the money is returned, there won't be a trip to Disneyland."

The class reacted angrily. "I sold a lot of candy bars for that trip," said Ken Matthews. Other people in the class nodded in agreement.

"We've been planning for months," said Pamela Jacobson.

"Yeah!" said Jerry McAllister. "What sort of creep would take our money?"

Ms. Wyler shook her head. "I'm really sorry about this," she said. "I thought the money would be safe in my locker." Everyone continued to grumble.

Elizabeth shot a sidelong glance at Jessica. She looked as upset as the rest of the class.

As soon as the bell rang, Elizabeth saw Jessica and Ellen Riteman huddle together and start whispering. Elizabeth wondered what the big secret was. When Elizabeth walked over to her, Jessica quickly straightened up. "What do you want?"

"Nothing," said Elizabeth. She stood there with

her arms wrapped around her books, not sure what to say next. "Isn't it awful about the class money?"

Lila Fowler came over. "Ooooh, Ellen," she said, "where'd you get those earrings? They're the same ones the lead singer in Toy Car has, right?"

Ellen pulled her hair away from her ears to reveal an elegant pair of gold-and-silver dangles. She looked at Jessica. "Uh, my aunt gave them to me," she said.

Lila shrieked. "You're so lucky. They're gorgeous. I saw a pair like them at the mall. They cost a fortune."

Ellen looked at Jessica again and smiled. "Georgio Fabio designed them," she said.

"Let's go, Ellen," said Jessica sharply.

Elizabeth watched as the two girls left the classroom and hurried down the hall. They were being so secretive all of a sudden. What were they up to? A horrible thought occurred to Elizabeth. It was a little strange that Ellen and Jessica had both shown up with expensive new things around the same time that the class money had disappeared. First Jessica's Walkman and now Ellen's earrings . . . Elizabeth shuddered at the thought. But she knew it was impossible. Jessica did some crazy things, but she would never steal. Elizabeth dismissed the thought from her mind.

"Earth to Elizabeth, earth to Elizabeth," said Amy, cupping her hands like a megaphone.

Elizabeth snapped back to reality. "Sorry," she said. "I was thinking about something."

"Time to put up posters," said Amy.

Ken was standing next to Amy. "I heard you needed someone tall," he said. He and Amy laughed. Ken was one of the shortest boys in the sixth grade.

Elizabeth followed Ken and Amy to the cafeteria entrance. "OK," said Amy. "I think this'd be a good place to put a poster."

Elizabeth nodded. While she and Amy held the poster in place, Ken taped it to the wall. "That's so rotten about the candy money," he said.

"I know," Elizabeth replied. Ken deserved to be angry, she thought. He'd probably sold more candy bars than anyone in the class.

Ken turned to Amy. "When's the last time you saw the money?"

"Last Tuesday," said Amy.

Ken tore off a piece of tape. "So sometime between last Tuesday and this Tuesday the money disappeared, right?" he said.

"Last Tuesday and today," said Amy. "I hadn't added yesterday's money yet."

"Why not?" said Ken.

Amy narrowed her eyes. "Because I forgot, Ken," she said. "Do you mind?"

Ken finished putting up the last piece of tape. "I just can't believe that a big cigar box like that could disappear," he mused. "First of all, it was inside Ms. Wyler's locker, inside the faculty room. No one's even allowed in there unless they have permission."

Amy fidgeted uncomfortably. What was Ken trying to say?

Elizabeth cut in. "But everyone knows that Ms. Wyler keeps her locker key in her desk," she said. "Anybody could have taken it and gone into the faculty room when no one was watching."

"I guess," said Ken.

Amy grabbed the stack of posters. "C'mon," she said. "We've got a lot more to do." She stomped into the cafeteria.

"What's wrong?" said Ken, catching up to her.

"Nothing," said Amy. "Just forget it."

Outside the Ritemans' house Mark was riding his bike in a large circle and thinking. Something strange was going on. It had been several days since he, Ellen, and Jessica had found the metal box, but the girls still hadn't told anyone. And when Mark started to tell his parents about it during dinner, Ellen had kicked him under the table. Later she said he shouldn't say anything because she and Jessica didn't want to return the letters to their original owner. He couldn't understand it. What was the big deal about a bunch of letters?

Mark stared down the street. Ellen wouldn't be home from school for another fifteen minutes. Maybe now was his chance. He parked his bike and ran inside. Seconds later he was sitting on Ellen's closet floor, examining the chest.

Inside, everything looked the same. He picked up the packet of letters, took out the first one, and started to read. Yuck. This was the one that Jessica and Ellen had gotten all mushy over.

He stuck the letter back in its envelope and opened the next one. It was hard to decipher the handwriting, but he managed to get through it. By the fourth letter Mark started to feel discouraged. Who cared about this mushy stuff anyway? "Dearest Jane," the letter began, "I've saved this money so that we might begin a life together. I know $200 may not seem like a fortune to you, but it's enough to get started."

Mark stopped. What two hundred dollars? He hadn't remembered this letter. Could this be what Jessica and Ellen were hiding? The front door slammed.

"Anybody home?" called Ellen.

Mark squeezed himself into the back of the closet. If Ellen caught him in there, he'd be dead. He could hear her running up the stairs.

"I guess nobody's here" she said. She walked into her room and slammed the door.

"Guess not," said someone else.

Mark strained his ears. It was Jessica!

"How much were those earrings?" said Jessica.

"Fifty-five dollars," said Ellen. "Thanks for reminding me. I can't let Mom see them or she'll ask where I got them."

Mark heard the dresser drawer open and close. "There!" said Ellen. "She'll never find them."

"Do you think we should have told Mark about the money?" said Jessica.

"Why should we?" said Ellen. "He's just a little kid."

Mark stiffened. He hated to be called a little kid.

"But he's pretty good about keeping secrets," said Jessica.

"He is not!" said Ellen. "Remember when I told him that I liked Travis Taylor and he swore not to tell anyone?"

"Oh, yeah," said Jessica. "You're right. Besides, we'd have to share the money with him."

Inside the closet, Mark shifted quietly. So there *had* been something more than love letters. He knew it!

"I'm going to change," Ellen said.

Mark panicked. He squeezed himself as far back as he could and held his breath. The closet door opened.

"What should I wear?" said Ellen. She rattled a few hangers.

"How about your white-and-purple sweat-shirt?" said Jessica.

Mark stared at Ellen's knees.

"Nah," said Ellen. "I don't like it anymore." She pulled something else off a hanger. "Where are my tennis shoes?" she said suddenly.

Mark felt Ellen's hand grope across the closet floor. She grabbed his sneaker and stopped. Mark's heart started to pound.

"What's this?" cried Ellen. She thrust back the hangers and revealed Mark.

"Oh, hi, Ellen," he said.

Ellen grabbed his shirt and pulled him out of the closet. "You little brat," she screamed. "You were spying on us, weren't you?"

Mark squirmed uncomfortably. "Let go of me," he said.

Ellen noticed the open treasure chest. "What have you been doing in here?" she said.

"You're ripping my shirt," said Mark. "Leave me alone."

Jessica gasped. "He must've heard what we were talking about."

Ellen tightened her grip. "What did you hear?"

Mark was getting angry. "Nothing," he said. "Just leave me alone."

"Not till you tell us what you heard," she said.

Mark howled. He'd had enough. "Everything!" he yelled, wriggling free of his sister's grip. "And if you don't give me my share of the money, I'm telling Mom."

Ellen stopped. "You wouldn't dare," she said slowly.

Mark didn't move. "Wanna bet?"

Ellen looked at Jessica. "Mark Riteman," she said, "if you say one word, you're going to regret it for the rest of your life."

Mark clenched his fists. "Then give me my money," he said.

Ellen tried to grab Mark's shirt again. "Help," he screamed. He ran down the hall to his room, slammed the door shut and locked it.

Ellen chased him, then pounded her fists on the door. "Open up!" she shouted.

"Never," said Mark. "Not in a million years. Give me my money or I'm telling Mom."

Ellen stopped pounding. "You'll be sorry," she said. "Just wait." She stormed back to her room and slammed the door. "Don't worry, Jessica," she said breathlessly. "I have a plan."

Elizabeth walked slowly up the street. With Ken's help, putting up the posters had taken no time at all. She was home from school much earlier than she'd expected. Suddenly she remembered her campaign speech. Maybe this would be a good time to work on it, even though Amy wasn't around.

Speeches were scheduled for next week, and she still had no idea what she was going to say.

Elizabeth walked in the front door. "Anybody home?" she called.

There was no answer.

She took a can of soda from the refrigerator and then sat down at her desk. She turned on her typewriter and inserted a clean sheet of paper. "My name is Elizabeth Wakefield, and I'm running for student council treasurer," she typed. "I think you should vote for me . . ." She glanced at Jessica's room and frowned. Had Jessica remembered to get back her sweatshirt? She finished the sentence. ". . . because I'll do a good job." Elizabeth made a face. "Yuck," she said. "Too stuck-up." She backed up the typewriter carriage and put x's over what she'd just typed. She stared at Jessica's room again. Maybe she'd better go look for the sweatshirt.

She stood up, walked into Jessica's room, and opened her closet door. On the floor were the shopping bags Jessica had carried home the other day. Several brand-new pairs of knee socks and a pale orange-and-purple sweatshirt hung out of one of the bags. Why hadn't Ellen come to pick them up? Elizabeth pushed the clothes aside and was surprised to discover Jessica's box of candy bars on the floor of the closet. Hadn't Jessica given Ms. Wyler five dollars? Why was the box still full? Elizabeth picked up the shopping bags again. She gasped. Inside one of the bags was a receipt for a Walkman.

Suddenly Elizabeth felt sick. Jessica hadn't found the Walkman at all. Where had Jessica gotten the money? With an anxious sigh she flopped down on Jessica's bed. *Stay calm,* she told herself. Jessica wasn't the type of person who would steal. There had to be a good explanation for all this.

Elizabeth took a deep breath and tried to think clearly. There must be an easy solution. Maybe she didn't hear it correctly. She'd simply ask Jessica again where she'd gotten the Walkman. She was sure Jessica would tell her the truth. Elizabeth stared down at a pile of clothes next to the bed. She retrieved her sweatshirt from the bottom of the heap. Elizabeth tried to smile as she headed back to her room. By tonight this whole thing would be all straightened out, she told herself.

Four

◇

Mark leaned his ear against the door and listened. Ellen had finally stopped pounding. Down the hall there was some whispering and then silence. What were Jessica and Ellen up to?

Mark stared at his clock. How long would he have to wait before he could exit his room safely?

"See you later, Ellen," he heard Jessica say. The front door slammed shut. He wished his mother would hurry up and come home.

At last Mark heard a car pull into the driveway. "Hi, kids," called Mrs. Riteman.

Mark slowly opened his door. The coast was clear. He raced down the stairs. "Mom," he yelled. "Me and Ellen and Jessica found buried treasure in the backyard. Ellen and Jessica said there was nothing in it but there was two hundred dollars and they took it." He took a deep breath.

Mrs. Riteman blinked. "What?" she said.

Mark pointed upstairs. "Ellen stole two hundred dollars," he repeated. "Go ask her."

Mrs. Riteman put down her bag and marched upstairs.

Ellen was lying on her bed, reading the latest issue of *Today's Stars*.

"Young lady," said Mrs. Riteman, "what's this I hear about some stolen money?"

Ellen sat up and put down her magazine. "What stolen money?" she said innocently.

Mrs. Riteman looked at Mark.

Mark ran to Ellen's closet. "I'll show you, Mom," he said. He pulled back Ellen's clothes. There was nothing on the floor except a few pairs of shoes. Mark frantically dug through Ellen's things, trying to find the metal box.

Ellen lifted one eyebrow and yawned. "Mark," she said, "*what* are you talking about?"

Mark remembered the earrings. "She's hiding some earrings in her dresser," he said. He pulled open the top drawer and started pulling out Ellen's socks and underwear.

"Do you mind?" said Ellen.

"Mom," Mark wailed. "No fair. Ellen found two hundred dollars, and now she's pretending she didn't."

Mrs. Riteman looked at Ellen and frowned. "Did you find some money and not tell anyone?" she said.

Ellen's eyes opened wide. "No, Mom," she said. "I swear. I don't even know what Mark is talking about."

Mark slammed his fist down on Ellen's dresser. "You are a liar," he said. "Liar, liar, liar."

Ellen calmly picked up her magazine. "Mom," she whispered, "I think Mark's been eating too much sugar. It's causing him to hallucinate."

Mark clenched his fists. "Ha, ha. Very funny," he said. "Just you wait. I'm going to find that treasure box and prove it."

Ellen lay back on her pillow and opened her magazine. "Whatever you say, Mark," she said.

Elizabeth rubbed her eyes and leaned over her typewriter. "So I hope you all vote for me for student council treasurer," she typed. "Thank you." She pulled the speech out of her typewriter and read it once more. It was OK, but nothing special. Tomorrow she'd show it to Amy.

Elizabeth heard the front door slam and then saw Jessica hurry by carrying a box of some kind. She waited several minutes and knocked on Jessica's door.

"Come in," Jessica shouted. She was listening to her Walkman and trying on the clothes Elizabeth had seen in the shopping bags earlier. "Do you think these shoes go with these socks?" she asked Elizabeth.

Elizabeth stared at the clothes. "Aren't those Ellen's?" she said.

Jessica looked surprised. "She told me I could borrow them anytime," she answered quickly.

Elizabeth wasn't sure how to begin. "How do you like your new Walkman?" she finally blurted.

"Fine," said Jessica. She turned abruptly. "What about these shoes instead?" she said.

Elizabeth sighed. Jessica wasn't making this easy. "Jess," she said, "are you going to tell me where you really got that Walkman?"

Jessica swallowed. "I *did* tell you," she said. "I found it on a bench at the mall."

"Are you absolutely, positively sure?" said Elizabeth.

"Of course," said Jessica. "Why?"

"How come you turned in five dollars for candy money and you still haven't sold any of your candy bars?" Elizabeth demanded.

Jessica bit her lower lip. "Uh, because Ellen and I were working together," she said. "We sold all of Ellen's candy bars first, and then we were going to sell mine."

Elizabeth stared at her sister.

"Really," said Jessica. She looked away.

Elizabeth couldn't tell whether Jessica was lying or not. She seemed to have a pretty good excuse about the candy bars, but still . . . "Jess," said Elizabeth, "I found a receipt for the Walkman in one of those shopping bags."

"I know," said Jessica, not missing a beat. "I found the *whole* package on the bench. Someone else bought the Walkman."

"If you're making any of this up, there's still time to return the money," said Elizabeth.

"What money?" said Jessica, looking confused.

Elizabeth began to wonder if she'd made a mistake. She looked at Jessica's Walkman.

"I told you," said Jessica firmly. "I found the Walkman at the mall. On a bench outside Casey's Place." She did a pirouette in the mirror. "I think these shoes look better," she said. She turned up the volume on her Walkman and began to dance. "I love this song," she shouted.

Elizabeth frowned. "Where did you say you found the Walkman?" she said.

Jessica pulled off her headphones and stopped dancing. "Uh, Casey's?"

Elizabeth shook her head. "Oh, Jess! Last time you said Sweet Valley Fashions."

Jessica grimaced. "I did?" She looked wildly around the room. "Oh, well, maybe that was it," she said. "I can't remember." She stuck her headphones on and started dancing again.

Elizabeth sighed. Why wasn't she telling the truth? Even if she hadn't taken the class money, she still couldn't explain the Walkman. And what about the way she and Ellen were so secretive? And Ellen's new earrings! Elizabeth walked back to her room and sat down on her bed. She had never been more disappointed in her twin in all their twelve years.

The next morning the Unicorns were huddled in a little group outside the cafeteria, whispering and giggling. Jessica hurried over to join them. "It's about time," said Janet.

"I overslept," said Jessica. "Sorry."

Janet lowered her voice. "OK, everyone," she said. "Follow me to the girls' bathroom."

The Unicorns looked like a small flock of purple birds as they tiptoed into the bathroom. Five minutes later they emerged wearing white sneakers with brown socks.

Bruce Patman, the cutest boy in the seventh grade, was the first to notice. "Look," he said. "Peter DeHaven clones."

"It's the new fad," said Janet with a straight face. "What do you think?"

"I think it's ugly," said Bruce. He started to laugh.

Janet stuck her nose in the air. "You obviously have no taste, Bruce Patman," she said. She strode up the hall, with the rest of the Unicorns giggling and trailing behind her.

At the other end of the hall Amy was taping up one of Elizabeth's posters which had fallen down. She saw the Unicorns walking toward her wearing smug expressions and brown socks. "That's not very nice," she said.

Janet stopped. "What do you mean?" she replied.

Amy's eyes narrowed. "It's not nice to make fun of people," she said.

Janet turned to the other Unicorns. "We're not making fun of anyone, are we?" she said. "We're starting a new trend." The Unicorns nodded in agreement.

Amy didn't answer.

Janet paused. "I hear your class isn't going to Disneyland," she said. "Someone stole the money."

Amy glared at Janet. "That's right," she said.

"Weren't you in charge of the money?" said Janet.

Amy swallowed. "Yes."

Janet nodded. "Hmm." She started up the hall again, the rest of the Unicorns trailing behind her. "Bye-bye, Amy."

Amy watched the Unicorns file past. She felt a tight little knot in her stomach. How dare Janet imply that she took the money! She glanced around the hall. Several people were standing in little groups, whispering. Amy was sure they were talking about her.

Just then Ken walked over. "Hi, Amy," he said.

"Hi," Amy mumbled.

"I was wondering," said Ken. "Do you think maybe you could have accidentally taken the cigar

box out of Ms. Wyler's locker and left it on the floor
or something?"

Amy stared at Ken.

"What's the matter?" he said.

Amy felt tears start to well up in her eyes.
"Nothing," she blurted. She ran into the bathroom
and locked herself into a stall. She couldn't believe
that anyone would actually think she'd taken the
class money.

Elizabeth was sitting in Mr. Bowman's room
with Julie Porter, when Caroline Pearce burst
through the door. Caroline had the biggest mouth in
Sweet Valley and wrote the gossip column for *The
Sweet Valley Sixers*.

"Did you see what the Unicorns are wearing?"
she said. "Brown socks and white sneakers." She
giggled.

Julie looked at Elizabeth. "Good thing Mr. Bowman doesn't wear sneakers," she said. Mr. Bowman
was Elizabeth's English teacher. His taste in clothing
wasn't so good either.

"Did Peter see the Unicorns?" asked Elizabeth.

Caroline nodded. "He pretended not to notice,"
she said. "But I could tell his feelings were hurt."

A typical Unicorn prank, thought Elizabeth. The
tricks they played was one reason she never liked the
Unicorns.

Mr. Bowman strolled over. "How's the election
issue coming?" he asked.

"Good," said Elizabeth. "We decided to print
the speeches and pass out the paper the day before
the election."

"Great idea," said Mr. Bowman. "Keep up the good work." The class bell rang, and Elizabeth slipped into her seat. "OK, class," said Mr. Bowman. "Let's get out a clean sheet of paper and do a little free association."

Everyone except Elizabeth groaned. This was one of Mr. Bowman's favorite exercises. Everyone was supposed to take a blank sheet of paper and write whatever came to mind.

Elizabeth smiled. She was probably the only person in the class who enjoyed doing the free association exercise. She started to write furiously. To her surprise, the first thing she wrote was "Is Jessica a thief?" She stared at her paper uncomfortably. She realized that she needed to talk to someone about this huge problem, but who? She wrote a few more sentences. "Dear Abby. I am a twelve-year-old girl. I have a twin sister who I think stole some money, but every time I try to bring it up, she changes the subject. What should I do? I don't want to accuse her unless I'm really positive. Signed, Confused." Elizabeth sighed.

"OK, class," said Mr. Bowman. "Time's up."

Elizabeth crumpled her sheet into a little ball. She felt a tiny bit better now.

Elizabeth had promised to show Amy her speech that day during lunch. The two girls found an empty table in the corner of the cafeteria and sat down. Amy seemed quieter than usual. "Anything wrong?" asked Elizabeth.

Amy poked at her Sloppy Joe. "I never know how to eat these things," she said. She tried to take a bite, but the filling oozed out onto her plate. "See what I mean?" she said. She threw the sandwich down in disgust.

"Amy, what's really the matter?" said Elizabeth.

Amy stared unhappily at her sandwich. "Everyone thinks I stole the money," she blurted. "Even Ken." Her eyes began to fill with tears again.

Elizabeth put her arm around Amy's shoulder. "Amy!" she said. "Don't say that. It's not true!" She glanced uncomfortably across the room. Jessica and Ellen were whispering again. Elizabeth watched Ellen's earrings bob up and down. She took a deep breath. "Amy," she said, "if someone you knew was really broke, and then suddenly that person and her friend showed up with some brand-new things and no explanation, what would you think?"

Amy wiped her eyes. "I'd wonder where they got the money," she said.

Elizabeth hurried on. "And what would you do if you asked them about it and they ignored you?"

"I'd think they were hiding something," said Amy. She stared across the room and saw Jessica and Ellen huddled together. Suddenly it hit her. She knew exactly who Elizabeth was talking about.

Elizabeth watched Amy's face grow angry. She realized she may have made a horrible mistake. What if Jessica and Ellen were innocent? "Amy, I'm not really sure—" she began.

But it was too late. Amy jumped up.

Elizabeth panicked. "Where are you going?" she said.

Amy silently walked past the Unicorns' table. She could feel her cheeks burning. She stalked over to the next table and put her tray down beside Caroline Pearce's. "You'll never believe what I just found out," she said.

Caroline leaned over. "Tell me," she said.

Five

Jessica sat on the steps outside the front entrance to the school. Everyone was heading home, but Jessica had promised Ellen she would wait for her. Jessica reached into her book bag and pulled out her Walkman. As she listened to a Johnny Buck song, she swayed to the beat of the music and tapped her foot.

She noticed Charlie Cashman and Jerry McAllister walk slowly by. Charlie whispered something to Jerry and then they both stared at her. Jessica looked down at her outfit. Was there something wrong?

Sophia Rizzo and Nora Mercandy hurried past. When they saw Jessica, they both gave her dirty looks.

Jessica squirmed uncomfortably. Why was everyone looking at her? She was relieved when she saw Ellen's cheerful wave. She jumped up and pulled off her headphones. "It took you long enough," she said.

Ellen handed Jessica her earrings. "Here," she said. "Take these before I forget."

Jessica stuck the earrings into her book bag.

She'd been keeping them at her house with the metal box. "Do you notice anything funny about me?" Jessica asked.

Ellen stared at her. "No. Why?"

"Because everyone's looking at me," said Jessica. She glanced up and noticed two seventh-grade boys pointing.

Ellen glared at the boys. "Why don't you take a picture?" she shouted. "It lasts longer." The boys moved away abruptly. Ellen turned to Jessica. "Want to go to the mall?" she said. "This school is giving me the creeps."

The two girls slowly headed downtown to the Valley Mall. It was another perfectly cloudless California afternoon so they decided to walk. In the distance the girls could see the Pacific Ocean shimmering brightly.

"How much money do you have left?" Ellen asked as they strolled along.

"Not too much," Jessica replied. "The Walkman, class trip money, knee socks, and sweatshirt almost cleaned me out. I think I'm going to try and save the rest."

"Me too," said Ellen. They walked together in silence. "Mark is really mad at me," Ellen finally said. "You may have to keep the chest and earrings at your house forever."

Jessica sighed. "Maybe we should have told him," she said.

"It's too late now," said Ellen. She avoided Jessica's gaze.

"I was thinking," said Jessica. "What happens if the owner of the chest comes to get it? What do we say?"

"I don't know," said Ellen. She stared ahead at the mall. "No one will claim it," she said at last. "It's been so long."

That night Jessica had a lot of trouble sleeping. She dreamed that the girl in the picture had come back to get the chest. In the dream the girl was an old woman now. "You stole my money," the woman said, glaring at Jessica.

"No!" cried Jessica. She tried to run away, but the old woman grabbed her arm and held on with her long, bony fingers. "Help!" screamed Jessica. She awoke with a start and stared at her arm. What if something like that were to really happen?

Jessica got out of bed, tiptoed down to the kitchen, and poured herself a glass of orange juice. As she sat quietly in the eerie darkness, she had another terrible thought: What if the woman were buried in Ellen's backyard next to the chest! That would make them both grave robbers! They could be arrested and thrown into jail. Jessica gulped down the rest of her juice and hurried back to bed. She slid as far as she could under the covers. Outside, a tree branch tapped steadily against the side of the house. Jessica pulled her pillow over her ears and squeezed her eyes shut. It took her a long time to fall asleep.

By the next day practically everyone in Sweet Valley Middle School was talking about Jessica and Ellen. "I heard," whispered Brooke Dennis to Nora Mercandy, "that Ellen didn't really get those earrings from her aunt. They were one of a kind, and Caroline Pearce said the jeweler sold them to a young girl. For cash."

Nora nodded knowingly. "And what about Jessica's new Walkman? Do you really believe she found it?"

Brooke shook her head. "Poor Elizabeth," she said. "She must feel so embarrassed."

"If I were her, I'd say something, wouldn't you?" added Nora.

Brooke nodded. "Shh. Here she comes."

Elizabeth walked stiffly past. She felt terrible. Thanks to Caroline's big mouth the whole school was talking about Jessica and Ellen. Elizabeth knew that if she hadn't said anything to Amy, this never would have happened. She saw Peter DeHaven slide by and disappear into the boys' bathroom. Today he was wearing his white sneakers with thick cotton socks, the kind that everyone wore.

Elizabeth hurried on to history class. When she took her seat next to Amy, her friend didn't even look up.

After class Amy bolted for the door. "Amy, wait," Elizabeth called.

Amy stopped and turned around. "What do you want?" she said.

Elizabeth could feel her face turning red. "I have to talk to you," she said.

"I'm busy," said Amy.

Elizabeth ran after her. "I don't appreciate the fact that you're spreading rumors about certain people," she said.

Amy's face was set in a hard line. "They're not rumors," she replied.

Elizabeth grimaced. "We don't know that for sure," she said. "And besides, I told you something in confidence and you blabbed it to Caroline Pearce. You may as well have printed it in the newspaper."

Amy shrugged. "So?"

"So I thought I could trust you," said Elizabeth.

"Stop trying to defend your sister," Amy said loudly. "She's a thief and you know it."

Elizabeth's cheeks burned. Several people walking by slowed down to listen. "You can't prove it," she said helplessly. She ran over to her locker and threw it open. She rummaged through her things, pretending to look for something.

"Are you OK?" said someone behind her. It was Ken.

Elizabeth turned her head so Ken wouldn't see the tears in her eyes. It was all too much for her to take. She felt ashamed of Jessica and betrayed by Amy.

"Where's your next class?" asked Ken.

"English," mumbled Elizabeth.

Ken reached over and took Elizabeth's books. "Come on," he said. "I'll walk you there."

Elizabeth wiped her eyes. "Thanks," she said. She and Ken started down the hall. Out of the corner of her eye she could see Amy glaring at them both.

But Elizabeth ignored Amy. Right now she was just glad to have a friend.

At the other end of the building Jessica and Ellen sat hunched over their stools in art class. The teacher, Mr. Sweeney, had just asked everyone to pair up for a new project. Ellen leaned over and whispered in Jessica's ear, "Is everyone still treating you like you have leprosy?"

Jessica nodded glumly.

"Lila hasn't talked to me all day," Ellen said. "I don't get it." She glanced nervously around the room. "Yesterday Caroline asked me about the earrings. She wanted to know if they were the same pair she'd seen at the mall."

"This morning Brooke said she couldn't believe I found a Walkman," Jessica added.

Mr. Sweeney cleared his throat. "Students, please pay attention," he said. "This means you, Ms. Riteman."

Ellen stopped whispering and sat back.

"Now that we've done some drawing of faces we've seen in magazines, we're going to try drawing our partners.

Everyone groaned.

"Students, please," said Mr. Sweeney. "This is merely an exercise in observation. Please don't worry if your portrait isn't accurate. It took masters like Rembrandt years to perfect this craft."

Jessica quickly drew a long, thin face with beady eyes and short black hair. She added horns to the head and two long fangs to the mouth. Underneath it she wrote "Portrait of Mr. Sweeney by Jessica Rembrandt." She slid the picture over to Ellen.

Ellen began to giggle uncontrollably.

"Ms. Riteman," said Mr. Sweeney, "what's so amusing?"

"Nothing, Mr. Sweeney," choked Ellen. Her eyes began to water.

With her back to the teacher, Jessica looked cross-eyed at Ellen and stuck out her tongue. "No laughing," she whispered.

Ellen snorted out loud.

Mr. Sweeney put down his piece of chalk.

"Let's see what's got you two so entertained," he said.

Before Mr. Sweeney could reach their table, Ellen grabbed the piece of paper and stuffed it under her sweater.

"Ellen!" exclaimed Jessica. Several people started laughing.

Mr. Sweeney held out his hand. "Hand it over," he said. The class snickered. Soberly, Ellen removed the drawing. Mr. Sweeney spread it on the table and studied it for several seconds. Then he crumpled it up and threw it into the wastebasket. "In the future, Ms. Wakefield," he said, "please try to spend more time listening and less time amusing Ms. Riteman."

No one in the class said a word. Jessica stared at the table. She didn't dare look at Ellen.

Mr. Sweeney clapped his hands together. "Now then," he said briskly, "where were we?"

Later that afternoon Amy was on her way to booster practice when Ken stopped her in the hall. "Hi, Amy," he said.

"Hi," said Amy without stopping.

Ken followed her down the hall. "Is something the matter?" he asked.

Amy knew she shouldn't let it bother her, but it did. "Why did you walk Elizabeth to class?" she blurted.

Ken looked at Amy in surprise. "Because she was upset," he said. "She's your best friend, and I don't think you treated her very nicely."

Amy turned angrily. "Since when is that your business, Ken?" she said.

"It *is* my business," he replied.

Amy stared at Ken. Why was he defending Elizabeth? A horrible thought occurred to her. What if Ken was doing this because he liked Elizabeth! Now Amy's face turned red. Without another word she rushed off to the gym.

All during booster club practice Amy thought about her conversation with Ken. On the other side of the gym she could hear the basketball team practicing. Everything was starting to make sense now—the way Ken had been so nice to Elizabeth when they were putting up posters the other day, the way he smiled at Elizabeth when they were together. Amy heard Janet, the booster captain, calling her name.

"What's with you today?" said Janet. "You've been late starting every single cheer."

Amy looked down the long line. "Sorry," she said. She tried to concentrate.

At the other end of the squad Jessica and Ellen were dragging their pompoms through the next routine. Amy gritted her teeth and did a forward flip. "Go Sweet Valley," she shouted, right on cue. She peeked over at Ken. If only she could get him to like her again. She felt herself getting angrier and angrier with Elizabeth. There must be something she could do, she thought. Maybe if there were some way to make Ken jealous . . .

After practice Amy hurried to Mr. Bowman's room. Elizabeth and Julie were still there, working on the paper. "Listen, Elizabeth," said Amy coldly. "I've decided I can't be your campaign manager anymore. I don't think the student council treasurer should have a thief for a sister."

Elizabeth looked shocked. "But—"

"I'm sorry," Amy interrupted. She turned on her heel and walked out the door.

In the library Amy found Peter hunched over a stack of albums in the record corner. He was wearing a pair of oversized earphones and intently reading one of the jacket covers. Amy pulled up a chair and sat down beside him. Peter looked up abruptly. "Hi, there." Amy grinned. "What are you listening to?"

Peter pulled off the earphones. "Johnny Buck," he replied.

"Johnny Buck?" said Amy.

Peter gave a serious nod. "I collect his albums. I've got them all." He stuck the earphones back on and began mouthing the lyrics. He knew the song by heart. His timing was perfect.

"That's not bad, Peter," said Amy.

He smiled and tapped his foot.

Amy looked down at his sneakers. "Nice shoes," she said. "They look much better with white socks too."

"Thanks," said Peter. He banged his ballpoint pen against the library cart and kept time with the record.

Amy pushed her chair closer. "Uh, Peter," she said. "Could I interrupt you for a minute?"

Peter lifted up the record needle.

Amy took a deep breath. "I was wondering," she said. "Have you ever thought about having a campaign manager?"

Six

◇

Elizabeth sat quietly by herself on the "thinking seat," a low branch of the large pine tree in the Wakefields' backyard. She just couldn't understand what had happened that afternoon with Amy. Why was Amy being so hateful toward her? *She* hadn't stolen the money. She didn't even know about it. And why was Amy so eager to spread rumors about Jessica and Ellen?

Elizabeth leaned back and stared up through the branches overhead. For her the thinking seat was the most peaceful spot in Sweet Valley. Whenever Elizabeth felt unhappy or confused, she would come here and try to sort out her feelings.

Elizabeth thought about the class money. That morning she'd seen Jessica take Ellen's earrings off her dresser and put them in her book bag. Why would Jessica be keeping the earrings unless she and Ellen didn't want Mrs. Riteman to find them?

Elizabeth rested her head against the tree and closed her eyes. She wished she could just erase the past few days and start over again.

Elizabeth heard the back door slam and felt

someone shake the tree branch. "Lizzie!" cried Jessica. "You won't believe what happened today in art class."

Elizabeth opened her eyes and peered up at Jessica's grinning face.

"Mr. Sweeney wanted us to draw portraits of our partners, and I had Ellen, only I drew this picture of Mr. Sweeney with fangs instead and Sweeney caught us. Then Ellen put the picture under her sweater but she wasn't quick enough." She began to laugh hysterically.

Elizabeth smiled faintly.

Jessica stopped laughing and looked closely at Elizabeth's face. "Have you been crying?" she asked.

Elizabeth didn't say anything.

Jessica crawled into the tree and sat down next to Elizabeth. "What's the matter, Lizzie?" she asked.

Elizabeth burst into tears. "Amy quit as my campaign manager," she said.

Jessica shrugged. "Is that all?" she said. "Gee, Lizzie. You had me worried there for a minute. I thought something was really wrong." She brushed her hands and started to climb back out. "Maybe Julie will help you out."

Elizabeth's anger started to rise. "You don't seem to understand, Jessica," she said evenly. "No one is going to vote for me anymore."

"Why not?" said Jessica. "They sure aren't voting for Peter." She laughed nervously. Something in Elizabeth's tone made her hesitate.

Elizabeth clenched her jaw. She'd had enough. "No one thinks the student council treasurer should have a thief for a sister," she said through gritted teeth.

Jessica's eyes opened wide. "You don't mean *me*?" she said incredulously.

"You're the only sister I have!" Elizabeth snapped.

"But what did I do?" said Jessica.

Elizabeth sighed. "You and Ellen stole the class money, didn't you?" she said. "Admit it, Jess."

"We *what*?" Jessica screamed. At that moment she realized why everyone had been staring at her and ignoring her. Jessica threw her hand across her heart. "Elizabeth, I swear I didn't take that money."

Elizabeth turned away.

"Elizabeth!" wailed Jessica. "How could you think I'd do something like that? Your own sister? Your own flesh and blood?"

Elizabeth stared stonily at her sister. "Then where did Ellen get those earrings?" she said. "And what about the Walkman? I know you're lying about finding it at the mall, Jessica. Don't deny it."

Jessica swallowed. "I'm not," she said. "And I promise I didn't take the class money."

"Give me a break," said Elizabeth. "Everyone in the class knows you're guilty, and I'm sick and tired of taking the blame for defending you. Why don't you just admit it?"

Jessica burst into tears. "You're wrong," she said, fleeing into the house.

Elizabeth wiped her eyes and stared after her sister. She heard the door slam. *It's true*, she thought sadly. *If Jessica had been innocent, she would have defended herself. But she couldn't*. Elizabeth closed her eyes and leaned back again. This was worse than any nightmare she had ever dreamed.

"Mom," said Jessica, "would you please ask Elizabeth to pass the butter?"

Mrs. Wakefield looked at her two daughters. Jessica and Elizabeth hadn't been talking to each other all afternoon.

"Elizabeth said you're a liar, too," Steven interrupted gleefully.

"I did not!" said Elizabeth.

"Steven," said Mr. Wakefield, "let's not aggravate the situation further." He cleared his throat. "Too bad you two aren't speaking," he said loudly. His eyes flashed mischievously. "I've got a secret to share with you both."

Jessica sat still. A secret! She stole a glance at Elizabeth. Elizabeth turned away. Jessica's curiosity was bursting. "What is it?" she said.

Mr. Wakefield shook his head. "I'm waiting for the right moment to tell you," he said.

Jessica's face fell. "Oh," she said, trying not to sound too disappointed.

Mrs. Wakefield started to clear the table. "I wish you two would tell me why you're not speaking to each other."

Elizabeth pursed her lips and turned her head. As long as Jessica wasn't talking, neither was she.

Steven rocked back in his chair. "I kind of like the quiet for a change," he said. "No jabbering. Nice and peaceful." He leaned across Jessica and helped himself to the rest of the green beans.

Jessica folded her arms and stared at Steven.

"Ha, ha," she said. "That's so funny I forgot to laugh." She shifted around in her seat and avoided looking at either one of her parents or Elizabeth. Things were starting to look bad for her. Maybe she and Ellen would have to change their story.

"May I be excused?" Elizabeth said. "I've got a lot of homework."

"Certainly," said Mrs. Wakefield.

Elizabeth carefully walked around the far end of the table so she wouldn't have to pass Jessica. Jessica picked up her half-eaten dinner and headed for the kitchen sink.

"Are you sure you're finished, Jessica?" asked Mrs. Wakefield.

"I'm not hungry tonight," Jessica replied.

The next morning Jessica waited anxiously outside the school building for Ellen. She'd had to walk to school by herself, since Elizabeth had sneaked out earlier. She saw Mary Robinson and Betsy Gordon, two seventh-grade Unicorns, heading in her direction. "Hi, you guys," she said, waving.

Mary and Betsy gave her cold stares and kept walking.

Jessica's heart sank. It was true! Everyone in the whole school thought she and Ellen had taken the money. Ellen came trudging through the parking lot, wearing a long face. Jessica ran over.

"I can't believe this," Ellen said. "You'd think I was contagious."

"I know," said Jessica. "It's awful." She reached into her book bag. "Want your earrings?" she asked.

"No, thanks," said Ellen. "I don't feel like wearing them today."

* * *

When Elizabeth had walked into Mr. Bowman's room that morning, no one was there yet—not even Mr. Bowman. Elizabeth put down her things and started to do some work on the election issue.

"Well, well," she heard Mr. Bowman say as he entered the room. "An early bird."

Elizabeth looked up and smiled. Mr. Bowman was wearing his loud plaid jacket again. Amy always said it made him look like a clown. Just thinking about Amy made Elizabeth wince.

"What are you doing here so early?" Mr. Bowman asked.

"I'm putting together all of the student council speeches," Elizabeth said. "I've gotten every one except for Peter's."

Mr. Bowman peered over Elizabeth's shoulder. "Very good." He picked up a piece of paper. "Yours?" he said.

"It's not too great," Elizabeth said.

"Mind if I read it?" said Mr. Bowman.

"OK," said Elizabeth. She pretended to fiddle around with the ditto masters while she waited for Mr. Bowman to finish.

"Sounds pretty good," he said, handing the speech back to her. "You might want to add a bit about why you think you're qualified for the job."

"But doesn't that sound stuck-up?" said Elizabeth.

"Not really," said Mr. Bowman. "It gives people confidence to know that they're voting for a qualified person."

Elizabeth nodded. Julie and Sophia burst

through the door. "Howdy, Mr. B," said Julie. She turned to Elizabeth. "Did you see Peter's new campaign posters?"

Elizabeth shook her head.

Julie grabbed her arm. "Come with me," she said. She pulled Elizabeth into the hall. Next to Elizabeth's poster another poster, twice as large, had been taped up. ROCKIN' PETER, it said in neon-orange letters. HE'S YOUR MAN. A generous amount of glitter had been sprinkled across the top.

Elizabeth looked at Julie and Sophia. "Rockin' Peter? Who thought that up?"

Julie pointed to the other end of the corridor. "Amy's working for Peter now."

Elizabeth stared down the hall. She could see Amy standing next to a cute boy in blue jeans. She did a double-take. It was Peter.

"Amy gave him a makeover," said Julie. "Can you believe it?"

Elizabeth's jaw dropped. The brown belt and brown pants were gone. In their place Peter had on some new jeans and a rumpled blue T-shirt that had a picture of the ocean on it. MAUI, it said in big black letters.

"He's kind of cute, don't you think?" said Julie.

"I guess so," said Elizabeth.

Peter and Amy started up the hall. There was a new bounce in Peter's walk, as if the clothes had somehow boosted his confidence. "Vote for Peter," Amy said as she handed out little handmade stickers with his name on them.

Elizabeth watched silently. Several other people had stopped to stare as well.

"Hey, Pete," shouted Charlie Cashman. "What happened to your clothes?"

Peter grinned good-naturedly. "I gave them to my sister," he shot back.

Charlie howled. "Not bad, DeHaven," he said.

Peter smiled.

"Are you going to vote for Peter?" interrupted Amy. She handed Charlie a sticker.

Charlie put the sticker on his shirt. "Sure. Why not?" he said. He grinned at Peter. "What did you say you're running for?"

That day in math class Jessica and Ellen sat by themselves in a far corner of the classroom, trying to look inconspicuous. "I'm sick of everyone giving us dirty looks," whispered Ellen.

Jessica peered gloomily around the room. "Me too," she said. "I wish we'd never found that buried treasure."

Ms. Wyler entered briskly. "Good day, class," she said. She opened her textbook. "Let's start today by going over our homework."

Class seemed to drag on forever. Jessica found it hard to pay attention. Finally the bell rang. As everyone got up to leave, Ms. Wyler said, "I'd like to see Jessica and Ellen at my desk, please."

The room suddenly became quiet as everyone turned to them.

Jessica gulped. She slowly collected her books and walked up to Ms. Wyler's desk. Ellen followed. No one else in the class moved.

Ms. Wyler waved her arm. "The rest of you can go," she said. She shuffled through her papers and acted as if nothing were the matter. "Go on, class," she said.

As soon as the last person left the room, Ms. Wyler walked over and shut the door. She returned to her desk and sat down. "I've heard something about you two and the class money," she said.

"It wasn't us, Ms. Wyler," Ellen burst in. "I swear on a stack of bibles."

Ms. Wyler frowned. "Then you know what I'm talking about?" she said.

Jessica's heart sank. Ms. Wyler must think they were guilty, she thought. "Ellen's right," Jessica said in her most convincing voice. "We would never take the class money. Never."

Ellen vigorously nodded her agreement.

Ms. Wyler flipped through a pile of papers. "I understand you both made some new purchases recently," she said. "A Walkman, a pair of earrings . . ."

Jessica looked at Ellen. "I *found* that Walkman at the mall," said Jessica. "On a bench near . . . Sweet Valley Fashions."

"And my aunt gave me the earrings," Ellen quickly added. "My Aunt Jackie. In Michigan. She's my dad's sister." Jessica gave her a nudge to shut up.

Ms. Wyler nodded. "I see," she said.

"Ms. Wyler, please," begged Jessica. "We're innocent. Really."

Ms Wyler looked at the girls. "As long as you tell me that you're innocent, I have no choice but to believe you," she said. "But if I find out otherwise, you'll have many, many people to answer to. Do you understand?"

"Don't worry, Ms. Wyler," said Ellen. She

shoved Jessica toward the door. "We're telling the truth."

Jessica and Ellen closed the door behind them, and Ellen leaned against the wall. "Great," she said. "She didn't believe one word. I'll bet she'll even call our parents. What do we do now?"

Seven

Later that same afternoon Elizabeth was about to go home when she noticed the campaign poster that she and Amy had hung earlier in the week. Someone had taken a black Magic Marker, crossed out the words ELIZABETH MAKES CENTS, and changed them to read JESSICA TAKES CENTS.

"Not very nice," observed Ken behind her.

Elizabeth turned around. "I'm beginning to feel like it's my fault about Jessica."

"Why?" said Ken. "I don't know anyone who's mad at you."

Elizabeth shook her head unhappily. "Amy is," she said. "She quit as my campaign manager."

Just then Amy and Peter walked out of the library. When Amy saw Ken and Elizabeth together, she began talking animatedly to Peter.

"Who's that with Amy?" said Ken.

"Peter DeHaven," said Elizabeth. "Amy's his new campaign manager. I guess she's trying to change his image."

Ken didn't say anything. He just kept staring at them.

"Are you OK?" Elizabeth asked.

Ken shrugged. "Sure," he said. He looked at Elizabeth. "When are the student council speeches?"

"The day after tomorrow," she said. She thought about her speech and how she was going to have to stand up in front of the whole school.

Ken continued to stand near Elizabeth. He kept glancing over at Amy, who was laughing hysterically at something Peter said.

"What position is Peter running for?" he asked abruptly.

"Treasurer," Elizabeth replied. "Against me."

Ken shuffled his right foot back and forth against the floor. "Oh."

Elizabeth took her ruined poster off the wall. "Guess there's no point in leaving this up," she said.

"Guess not," said Ken.

The next evening Jessica was lying on her bed, listening to her Walkman and singing along with Johnny Buck. "No one's been lonely as lonely as me," she crooned. "Why I'm alone is life's great mystery." She sighed and stared at the ceiling. *Johnny's right,* she thought. She'd never felt so abandoned. Even the Unicorns were avoiding her. She wondered if this was the way things were going to be for the rest of her life.

Mrs. Wakefield stuck her head in the door. "How's that homework coming?" she asked.

"OK, I guess," Jessica answered. She flipped open her math book and stared at the assignment. The truth was, she hadn't even started it. There'd been so much going on the past few days that she'd found it impossible to concentrate.

Jessica could hear Elizabeth practicing her student council speech in the next room. "Hello, my name is Elizabeth Wakefield, and I'm running for treasurer," she was saying. Jessica buried her head in her pillow. She wished she could ask Elizabeth for help with her homework, but she didn't dare.

Jessica heard Elizabeth get up from her desk and walk downstairs. A brilliant idea occurred to her. What if she just borrowed Elizabeth's homework without telling her? She could copy it and return it in the morning before Elizabeth ever noticed it missing.

Pleased with her plan, Jessica tiptoed through the bathroom that connected her room with Elizabeth's. The coast was clear. She dashed into her sister's room, snatched the notebook off her desk, and replaced it with her own, which was identical to Elizabeth's. Seconds later she was back in her room, copying the assignment. She didn't even blink when Elizabeth returned to her room. There was no way that Elizabeth would ever find out, she thought.

The next morning Elizabeth was up early. Student council speeches were scheduled for first period, and Elizabeth was already dreading them. She picked up her speech, read it over several more times, then stuck it inside her notebook for safekeeping.

Downstairs in the kitchen Elizabeth fixed herself a piece of toast and a glass of orange juice. She'd worn her favorite sweater, the pale blue one which showed off her blue-green eyes.

"Don't you look pretty," she heard her father say.

Elizabeth smiled. He was usually gone by the

time she made it downstairs. "Student council speeches are today," she said.

"Ah," said her father. "Good luck."

Upstairs Jessica was still tossing and turning in bed. She'd had another restless night and dreamed for hours about the girl in the picture. Her buzzing alarm clock woke her abruptly. Jessica sat up and rubbed her eyes. She could hear Elizabeth downstairs in the kitchen. "Uh-oh," she said suddenly. "Lizzie's notebook!" She reached under her bed, grabbed the notebook, and hurried through the bathroom. It only took a second to switch the notebooks, and by the time Elizabeth made it back upstairs, Jessica was already safe in her room.

Elizabeth threw her things into her book bag and hurried off. " 'Bye, everyone," she called. "Wish me luck!"

"Good luck," Mrs. Wakefield answered cheerfully.

Jessica smiled to herself and pulled on her sweater. Good thing she'd remembered the notebook. She was in enough trouble already.

Elizabeth sat on a folding chair on the side of the auditorium stage and watched the classes file in grade by grade. Her hands nervously clutched her notebook. On the other end of the stage she could see Amy giving Peter some last minute instructions. Today he had on another new T-shirt. This one was bright orange and said DAVEY'S SURF SHOP on it. His looks had certainly improved, Elizabeth thought, studying him more closely. She could even detect the faint beginnings of a tan.

Olivia Davidson, the presidential candidate,

leaned over to whisper in Elizabeth's ear. "Peter must be taking cute pills."

Elizabeth had mixed feelings about what was happening. On the one hand, it was good that Peter's image was improving. But still, she wished it wasn't at her expense.

The school principal, Mr. Clark, strode onto the stage. He picked up the microphone and tapped it a few times. "Testing, testing," he said. The microphone shrieked loudly. "OK, boys and girls," he said. "If I may have your attention, please."

Elizabeth looked out at the audience and suddenly felt sick to her stomach. She'd never spoken to this many people in her life. She clasped her hands together to prevent them from shaking, and then her knees weakened instead. She tugged on her skirt and took a few deep breaths.

"Nervous?" said Olivia.

Elizabeth nodded.

"Me too," said Olivia. "Don't worry, you'll do fine. Once you start talking, you forget about it."

Elizabeth smiled gracefully. She noticed that Olivia had neatly typed out her speech on index cards. Elizabeth opened her notebook to take out her speech. She frowned and flipped through the pages. And then she panicked. *I put my speech in my notebook this morning. Where is it?*

Mr. Clark was speaking to the audience. "We'll start the speeches by hearing from the presidential candidate."

Elizabeth searched through her notebook a second time. Where was her speech? She began to get desperate. It *has* to be here, she thought. She reached behind her chair and rummaged through her book bag. It wasn't there either.

Olivia got up and walked to the podium. The audience became quiet. Elizabeth saw all those staring faces. Her mind was a blur. What was she going to do? What was she going to say? There was no time to write it down again. She'd just have to remember what she could.

She heard Mr. Clark announce the next candidate and then the next. Finally she heard him say Peter's name. That meant she was next. Elizabeth looked at the clock. Maybe the bell would ring and she'd have to wait until tomorrow to give her speech. She squeezed her eyes shut and prayed that Peter would take his time.

From behind the stage came the sound of very loud rock music. Elizabeth saw Amy standing in the wings, operating a record player. At that moment Peter burst through the curtain wearing dark sunglasses. To the beat of the music he said, "I'm Rockin' Peter, and I'm here to say, if you vote for me, you'll do OK."

Elizabeth's jaw dropped. *This* was Peter's speech? The audience started to clap and cheer, but Peter wasn't finished. He spun around and bent the mike to the ground. "I want to help, you bet I do, so if you vote for me, I'll see you through. I'm rock, rock, rock, rockin' Peter." He leaned backward until it looked like he was going to fall over, and then he hopped across the stage.

"Go, Peter," someone shouted. Two sixth-grade boys stood up on their chairs and whistled.

Elizabeth watched in amazement. Peter was

really good. And funny too. The audience loved him.

Peter fell to his knees. "I'll watch your cash, I'll guard your stash," he was saying. He bounced across the stage again, this time on his knees. Elizabeth recognized a few of the Boosters' moves and saw Amy signaling directions from offstage. So *this* was what she and Peter had been up to! She couldn't help being impressed, even though she knew it was going to make things much worse for herself.

Finally the song was finished. It took forever for the audience to calm down. Elizabeth kept looking at the clock and hoping that the bell would ring. But when Mr. Clark finally took the microphone, there was just enough time left for her to do her speech.

Mr. Clark wiped the tears from his eyes. "Well," he said, "I can't remember when I've laughed so much at a campaign speech." He cleared his throat and the audience grew quiet. "We have one more speech scheduled for today," he said. "The other candidate for student council treasurer is Elizabeth Wakefield."

Elizabeth gulped and walked slowly to the podium. How was she ever going to follow Peter's act? She looked out at the sea of faces and smiled weakly. "I'm Elizabeth Wakefield and I'm running for student body treasurer," she began. The audience stirred restlessly. A big knot started to form in Elizabeth's throat. It just wasn't fair. "I think you should vote for me because . . ." Her voice quavered. "Because I'm very well-qualified for the job," she finished, taking a deep breath. Slowly, painfully, she was able to remember most of her speech, although it didn't sound the same as when she'd practiced it at home. After she sat down, there was a scattering of polite applause.

The bell rang and everyone immediately stood up. "Don't forget," called Mr. Clark as the students hurried out of the room. "Elections are tomorrow during lunch."

Elizabeth lowered her head and rushed out of the cafeteria, her cheeks still burning. "Lizzie!" she heard Jessica call.

Elizabeth kept walking until she reached the farthest stall in the girls' bathroom.

Jessica caught up to her. "Lizzie, what happened?" she said. "Your speech sounded so good when you rehearsed it at home."

Elizabeth was so grateful to see her sister that she forgot how angry she was with her. "Oh, Jess," she said. The tears started to roll down her face. "I was terrible, wasn't I? You won't believe what happened. I lost my speech." She blew her nose on a piece of toilet paper.

"How?" said Jessica.

Elizabeth shook her head. "I don't know," she said. "I put it in the front of my notebook this morning."

Jessica's face suddenly turned pale.

"What is it?" said Elizabeth.

"Nothing," Jessica replied quickly.

Elizabeth stared at her sister. "Are you sure?"

Jessica bit her lip. "Positive."

A look of horror crossed Elizabeth's face. "Jessica," she said slowly. "You wouldn't have my speech in *your* notebook, would you?"

Jessica gripped her book bag. "Of course not."

Elizabeth's eyes narrowed. "Let me see," she said.

Jessica hugged her book bag to her chest.

"I want to see," Elizabeth repeated.

Jessica knew she was cornered. "Lizzie, I didn't do it on purpose," she wailed. "I promise. You must have stuck the speech in my notebook by accident."

Elizabeth gritted her teeth. "How?" she asked.

Jessica swallowed. "Maybe when I borrowed your notebook to copy your math homework," she said in a tiny voice.

"Jessica!" howled Elizabeth. "What are you trying to do? Ruin my life?"

Several girls stopped talking and turned to watch.

Elizabeth's face got redder and redder. "You lied about the class money, and you stole my speech."

"I didn't," said Jessica. "That's not true."

Elizabeth shoved past her sister. "It is," she said. "Why don't you just leave me alone?"

Jessica leaned against the bathroom wall. Now she'd really blown it. "What are you staring at?" she said angrily to the other girls. Several of them whispered something and hurried out of the bathroom. "I'm not a thief," Jessica called after them. "I'm not."

Jessica found Ellen at the other end of the hall, getting some books out of her locker. "Ellen," she said. "We have to do something. Everybody hates us, and I've ruined Elizabeth's life. I'm giving you back the chest," said Jessica flatly. "I think we should tell the truth about the treasure."

Ellen swallowed. "But we'll have to return the

money," she said. "And we've already spent most of it."

"I don't care anymore," said Jessica. "I'll baby-sit. I'll walk Mrs. Bramble's dog. I won't spend my allowance for the next two years." She started crying. The class bell rang. "I'm coming over after school," Jessica said. "With the chest." She hurried off to class.

"Maybe we can think of something else," Ellen called after her.

"Forget it, Ellen," said Jessica. "It's not worth it anymore."

Eight

◇

Peter and Amy were having a hard time maneuvering their way through the crowded hallway. Every time they managed to gain a few feet, someone else came over to congratulate them. Now as they worked their way toward their classrooms, Amy saw Jerry McAllister approaching.

"Good work, DeHaven," said Jerry. He gave Peter a friendly slap on the back and pulled out his ballpoint pen. "Watch this." He put the pen up to his mouth like it was a microphone. "Rock, rock, rock, rockin' Peter," he crooned into his pen.

Peter grinned. He felt someone else tugging on his arm.

"You were fantastic," said Janet Howell. "I didn't know you were so talented."

"Thanks," he said.

Amy stood protectively by his side. "Did you want something, Janet?" she asked.

Janet gave Peter a big smile, the one all the Unicorns used if they wanted something. "I just had the best idea," she said. "I think Peter should perform with the Boosters at our next game." Her smile broadened. "What do you think, Peter?"

"Uh, I guess so," he said.

"You'd be really great," Janet continued enthusiastically. "We could have you do some of the cheers with us. Maybe we could even get you a special uniform."

"That's really nice of you, Janet," interrupted Amy, "but don't you think you're being a little hypocritical?"

"What do you mean?" said Janet.

"Only a few days ago you were making fun of Peter," said Amy.

Janet's face turned red. "That was before this," she replied in a huffy voice.

"Oh," said Amy. "I see."

Peter coughed. "I'd like to perform with the Boosters," he said. "It sounds like fun."

Janet beamed at him. "Oh, good," she said. "Then it's settled." As she walked away, she glared at Amy.

"Those Unicorns are so two-faced," muttered Amy.

Peter shrugged. "I guess that's the way some people are," he said. He quietly opened his locker and exchanged his books. "Thanks for helping me on my speech," he said, closing the door. "Those cheers really helped."

"That's OK," said Amy. "It was your talent that pulled it off."

Peter nodded thoughtfully. "Why did you switch from Elizabeth to me?" he asked suddenly. "I thought she was your best friend."

"Yes," said Amy.

"Her feelings must be hurt," Peter added.

"I'm sure she'll recover," said Amy, turning away.

"I always wanted a best friend," Peter said quietly. He stared at his new shoes. "Maybe now things will be different."

A wave of guilt swept over Amy. Maybe she *had* been a little mean to Elizabeth. And what about Peter? Hadn't she been just as bad as everyone else about making fun of him behind his back? The only reason she'd taken a real interest in him was to make Ken jealous. What sort of a friend did that make her? "I've gotta go, Peter," she blurted.

Amy's next class was cooking, and her partner was Ken. When she walked into the classroom, she was surprised to see Julie sitting next to Ken. They appeared to be having a serious conversation.

As Amy approached her seat, Julie stood up. "Sorry," she said. "Ken and I were just talking."

Amy watched Julie leave. "Hi," she said to Ken.

"Hi," said Ken. He bent over the comic book he was reading.

"How've you been?" said Amy.

Ken didn't even look up. "OK," he replied.

Amy's heart sank. What was the matter with Ken? Wasn't he supposed to be jealous? Why wasn't he happy to see her?

For the rest of the class Ken barely paid attention to Amy. She started to feel guilty about all her scheming. What had she done wrong?

After the final bell rang, Amy headed for Mr. Bowman's room. The election issue of *The Sweet Valley Sixers* had to be run off and stapled before tomorrow.

"Just in time," said Mr. Bowman as Amy came through the door.

"For what?" said Amy. She noticed Elizabeth standing over Mr. Bowman's desk. Her eyes were red and puffy, as if she'd been crying.

"I'd like you and Elizabeth to go to the supply closet in the faculty room and bring me two more boxes of mimeograph paper," he said. "Here's the key."

Silently, the two girls walked down the hall. When they reached the supply closet, Amy fiddled with the key for several seconds before managing to unlock it. "After you," she gestured politely.

"No. You go ahead," said Elizabeth.

Amy fumbled with the light switch and then stepped inside. The supply closet was actually a small room that had been lined with shelves from floor to ceiling. A lot of extra school supplies were kept there.

"I don't suppose you know where the mimeograph paper is," said Amy.

"Mr. Bowman said it's on the left side of the closet near the floor," Elizabeth replied. There was a strained silence as the girls bent down to look. "I found it," Elizabeth said finally. She started to pull out the boxes.

Outside, in the faculty room, Mr. Nydick, the social studies teacher, had come in to put up a sign about a teacher workshop. He noticed the door to the supply closet open and frowned. "Someone being careless again," he grumbled. He tacked up his sign and then walked over to the closet. With a loud grunt he flipped off the light and slammed the door shut.

"People should be more careful," he said as he turned and left the room.

Inside the closet Amy and Elizabeth suddenly found themselves in the dark. "Hey!" said Amy. "What happened?"

Elizabeth groped across the floor. "Someone must've thought there was no one in here," she said. She managed to find the light switch and turn it back on. She reached for the doorknob and tried to twist it. "Uh-oh," she said.

Amy hopped up. "Here. I have the key."

Elizabeth looked at her. "There's no keyhole on this side," she said.

"There has to be," said Amy.

Elizabeth stood back and watched Amy inspect the knob. "Now do you believe me?" she said.

Amy pounded on the door. "Open up," she shouted. "We're locked inside here."

"I don't think there's anyone in the faculty room right now," said Elizabeth. She folded her arms and sat down cross-legged on the floor, a resigned expression on her face. "We might as well wait it out."

Amy stared at Elizabeth. "What's the matter with you?" she said. "Don't you even care? We could die in here. We could run out of air and they wouldn't discover our bodies until tomorrow." She pounded on the door again. "Help. Let us out of here."

Elizabeth's eyes filled with tears. "It doesn't matter anymore," she said bitterly. "Nothing matters."

Amy sat down and put her arm around her

friend. "Yes, it does," she said gently. "We don't want to spend the rest of our lives in the supply closet."

Elizabeth burst into tears. "Why don't you like me anymore?" she said. "Was it something I did?"

Amy felt terrible. Peter was right. She had hurt her best friend's feelings. How would she ever make it up to her? "Elizabeth, I'm sorry," she said. "I didn't mean it. I wasn't thinking. I never planned to hurt you. It's just that I didn't want to take the blame for the class money anymore. And then when Ken started to like you, I guess I got jealous."

Elizabeth sniffled. "Ken?" she said. "Why were you jealous of Ken and me?"

"Because he likes you," said Amy. "I thought if I paid attention to Peter, Ken would get jealous and like me again. Only now Ken doesn't like me either," she said, thinking about cooking class. She leaned unhappily against the shelf. "I've really messed things up."

Elizabeth reached over and opened a box of tissues. She blew her nose and wiped her eyes. "You're imagining the whole thing, Amy. Just like you imagined that everyone was blaming you for taking the money. Besides, Ken told Julie today that you like Peter now."

"Peter!" exclaimed Amy.

"Why else would you be spending so much time with him?" said Elizabeth.

Amy realized what an awful mistake she'd made. She was about to lose her two closest friends, and all because she'd thought only of herself. If she hadn't been so selfish in the first place, she would never have told anyone Elizabeth's secret about Jessica.

"You took advantage of me, of Ken, of Peter, and of Jessica," said Elizabeth. "All because of what you imagined." She turned away. "And now Peter is probably going to win the election," she said finally. "Not that he doesn't deserve it," she added.

"I thought your speech was very good," said Amy.

Elizabeth made a face. "What speech?" she said. "It was sitting in Jessica's notebook the whole time."

"It sounded good to me," said Amy. "I liked when you told about your qualifications."

"You did?" said Elizabeth.

Amy nodded. "What can I do so we can be friends again?" she said. "I've missed you."

Elizabeth smiled. "Me too." She reached over and gave Amy a hug. "Friends," she said.

"Forever," Amy replied solemnly.

Elizabeth sighed and looked around the room. "Now how do we get out of this place?"

Amy pointed to the shelves. "Think we can find a saw in here?" she said.

"It's worth a try," said Elizabeth.

The two girls immediately began digging through the shelves. "I guess there's not much need for a saw in middle school," observed Amy after several minutes. "What time is it?"

"Four-fifteen," said Elizabeth. "Our only hope is that Mr. Bowman comes looking for us." On a large piece of construction paper she wrote HELP! WE'RE LOCKED IN THE CLOSET. She slid it underneath the door.

"That's got to work," said Amy. "Some teacher will show up eventually."

"Let's hope so," said Elizabeth. She sat back down on the floor. Over in the far corner she noticed a stack of things they hadn't looked through yet. "Maybe there's something we can use in that corner," she said. She took a pile of art smocks off the shelf and gasped. "I don't believe it," she said. Hiding behind the smocks were several old math posters and a familiar-looking cigar box.

"What is it?" said Amy. "A saw?"

Elizabeth pulled out the cigar box and flipped open the lid. "Better," she said.

Amy's jaw dropped. "The class money?" she said. "You've got to be kidding!" She and Elizabeth quickly counted the contents. "It's all here," said Amy. "Every single cent."

"Ms. Wyler must have accidentally stuck it there when she was putting away these posters," cried Elizabeth.

"And then it got buried behind the art smocks," Amy added.

Elizabeth closed the lid and looked directly at Amy. "Jessica wasn't guilty," she said.

Amy swallowed. "You're right."

Elizabeth sighed loudly. "I'm so relieved," she said. "Poor Jessica. No wonder she was so upset when everyone blamed her. Wait till I tell her."

Just then the girls heard a key in the lock. A

moment later the door to the closet opened. "Aha!" said Mr. Bowman. He held up Elizabeth's note. "I understand you're looking for a locksmith."

Amy and Elizabeth cheered, and then dashed out the door. "Fresh air," shouted Amy. "Thank you, thank you, Mr. B. You saved our lives."

"I wouldn't go that far," said Mr. Bowman.

Still clutching the cigar box, Elizabeth said, "We need to talk to Ms. Wyler right away. It's an emergency."

Mr. Bowman raised his eyebrows. "Very well," he said.

"And after that," Amy added, "we have to go to Elizabeth's house. We need to talk to somebody. The paper can wait until tomorrow."

Mr. Bowman looked at Elizabeth and then at Amy. He walked into the closet. "Did something strange happen in here?" he said.

Elizabeth and Amy laughed. "You could say that," said Elizabeth. She grabbed Amy's arm. "Come on, Amy," she said. "I can't wait to see Ms. Wyler's face."

When Elizabeth and Amy arrived at the Wakefields' about twenty minutes later, Steven was the only one around. "Where is everybody?" said Elizabeth.

Steven spooned marshmallow sauce onto his bowl of ice cream. "What do I look like?" he said. "A bulletin board?"

"This happens to be an emergency," Amy cut in.

Steven put a big spoonful of his sundae into his mouth. "What'll you pay me?" he said.

"Steven!" said Elizabeth. "We're not kidding."

Steven tilted back in his chair. "Dad's at the office," he said.

"And . . . ?" said Elizabeth impatiently.

Steven dipped his spoon into his ice cream and watched the marshmallow sauce drip over the edge of the bowl. "Mom said something about going to school to talk to one of Jessica's teachers."

"We know that," said Elizabeth. "Ms. Wyler said we'd just missed them. She'd called Mom and Mrs. Riteman in because of all the rumors going around. She wanted to check out Jessica and Ellen's story."

"So what else do you want to know?" asked Steven.

"Where is Jessica?" said Amy.

Steven grinned. "If I were Jessica, I'd be hiding out with Ellen." He tilted his chair forward again and chuckled to himself. "Boy, is she going to get it."

Elizabeth and Amy dashed out the door. "Not if we hurry, Steven," called Elizabeth. "Jessica and Ellen are innocent, and we've got the proof!"

Nine

◇

Jessica and Ellen sat on Ellen's front porch, waiting for Mrs. Riteman to get home from work. The treasure chest sat between them.

Jessica rested her elbow on the chest and sighed. "It's all for the best," she said.

"Right," said Ellen.

There was an uncomfortable silence. Neither girl was looking forward to telling the truth. "Do you think your mom is going to be mad?" said Jessica.

Ellen stared at the chest. "I'll probably be grounded for lying and for taking money that didn't belong to me," she said. "But I guess it's better to have one person mad at me than the whole school."

Jessica thought about what Ellen had said. If only they could think of some way to convince the class that they were innocent, and still keep the Walkman and earrings. "I have an idea," said Jessica. "What if we tell everyone that we found a buried chest and when we returned it to its owners, they gave us a reward?" She looked hopefully at Ellen.

"Do you think anyone would believe us?" Ellen said.

"It's possible," said Jessica.

"What would we do about Mark?" said Ellen.

Jessica frowned. "Maybe we could pay him some money to keep quiet." she said.

"I doubt it," said Ellen. "Besides, we'd have to hide the chest again." She paused. "And who would we say the chest belonged to?"

"Good point," said Jessica. She idly kicked her feet against the porch steps. "My mom's probably going to kill me for taking that money," she said finally. She thought about Elizabeth and all the trouble she'd caused her sister. "Maybe it's worth it, though," she added. She stared off into the distance and saw a young woman walking up the street. Jessica turned pale.

"What is it?" said Ellen.

The woman was closer now. She had dark hair and was very beautiful. She gazed at them and started in their direction. "It's her." Jessica gasped. "The girl in the picture."

Ellen watched in disbelief. "No," she said. "It can't be. She would be old now."

Jessica's eyes grew wide. "Ellen!" she said. "It's her ghost! She's come to get her things." She grabbed Ellen's arm.

Ellen leaned forward and strained her eyes. "Are you serious?" she said.

"It's exactly like my dream," Jessica replied earnestly. "I *knew* we shouldn't have taken that money. Now she wants it back."

Ellen stared at the figure moving silently up the street. She *did* look a lot like the photograph. Ellen moved closer to Jessica. "Can't we do something?" she whispered.

Jessica continued to squeeze Ellen's arm. "Go away," she called in a thin voice. "We didn't mean to take your money. Honest we didn't." Jessica had never felt more sorry. She was sorry she'd lied, sorry she'd bought the Walkman, even sorry she knew Ellen Riteman.

"We'll never do it again," Ellen added. "We promise."

The ghost kept walking. She reached the bottom of the Ritemans' driveway, stopped, and then continued up the walk. A faint smile crossed her lips.

"The chest," Jessica said under her breath. "Maybe she wants the chest."

Ellen grabbed the treasure chest and shoved it toward the ghost. "Here. Take it," she said. "We don't want it."

The ghost raised her eyebrows quizzically.

"We're really sorry about the money," Jessica added. "But the letters and the pictures are there just the way you left them. And we promise we'll return every cent of the money."

"Every cent," Ellen echoed.

The ghost looked puzzled. "I don't understand," she said. "There must be some mistake."

Jessica and Ellen huddled closer.

"Is this chest meant for me?" she repeated.

Jessica nodded, too frightened to speak.

"I'm Laura Wright," said the ghost. "My grandmother lived in this house."

Ellen and Jessica continued to stare.

"Her name was Jane McCreary," said the ghost. "She lived here as a girl. I just happened to be in

Sweet Valley on business and I wanted to come and visit the house."

Jessica leaned forward.

"Is anything the matter?" said the ghost.

It dawned on Jessica that maybe they'd made a mistake. A big mistake. "What did you say your grandmother's name was?" she asked.

"Jane," said the ghost. "Jane McCreary."

Slowly, Jessica released her grasp on Ellen's arm. "You're Jane's granddaughter?"

Laura laughed. "People say I resemble her." She smiled at the girls. "I hope I didn't frighten you."

Jessica and Ellen both took deep breaths.

Ellen opened the chest and pulled out the portrait of Jane. "You won't believe this, but we found this chest buried in the backyard a few weeks ago," she explained.

Laura examined the portrait. "That's Grandmother Jane," she said softly. She looked at the girls in amazement. "No wonder you two were acting so strange a minute ago. You must have thought I was Grandmother Jane. How in the world did you find this?"

Jessica and Ellen poured out the story about how they'd discovered the chest.

As Laura listened, she dug through the contents. "This is incredible," she said. "What an amazing coincidence."

Jessica and Ellen couldn't believe it either. They were dying to find out what had happened to Jane.

"Is your grandmother still alive," Ellen asked.

Laura shook her head. "She died about four years ago."

Jessica was just about to ask about William when she noticed her mother and Mrs. Riteman pull up in Mrs. Riteman's car. "Uh-oh," she said. "It's our moms, and they're together."

"Great," said Ellen.

The two mothers climbed out of the car, worried expression on their faces.

"Hi, Mom," Ellen called bravely. "Where've you been?"

Mrs. Riteman frowned. "With Ms. Wyler," she replied. She shut the car door. "We have some talking to do, young ladies."

"This is Laura," said Ellen. "Her grandmother used to live in this house. She's come back to see it, and you won't believe what happened."

Mrs. Riteman relaxed a little. "How lovely," she said. "If you'll forgive us, though, we really need to have a word with these two girls alone."

Jessica took a deep breath. "Mom, see this box?" she said. "We found it buried in the backyard a few weeks ago."

"Jessica," said Mrs. Wakefield, "please don't change the subject." She turned to Laura. "I must apologize," she said. "The girls are in a lot of trouble right now."

"But, Mom," Jessica interrupted, "this has to do with Laura. The box we found was full of letters to Laura's grandmother. Love letters." She threw open the chest and pulled out the packet of letters. "See?"

Mrs. Wakefield shook her head. "I still don't understand," she said.

Laura picked up the packet of letters and began reading them.

Mrs. Riteman looked sternly at Ellen. "Ms. Wyler told me you claimed that Aunt Jackie had sent you an expensive pair of earrings. Did she?"

Ellen shook her head. "No," she said quietly.

"Then what does finding some love letters have to do with this?" she demanded.

Jessica glanced at Ellen. They couldn't turn back now. "There was also two hundred dollars in that chest," she said, swallowing. "Laura's grandmother's boyfriend gave it to her so they could elope."

Laura looked up momentarily.

"And?" said Mrs. Wakefield.

Jessica gulped. "We split the money. I bought a Walkman and some clothes, and Ellen bought earrings," she said, staring at the ground. "We didn't think anyone would ever find out."

"So that's what Mark was trying to tell me!" said Mrs. Riteman. "He kept insisting he and the girls had found buried treasure."

"And the class money?" said Mrs. Wakefield.

"We didn't take that," said Ellen. "Everyone blamed us because of the Walkman and earrings."

Mrs. Riteman look dismayed. "Oh, Ellen," she said. "How could you take something that didn't belong to you?"

"We're going to return the money to Laura," said Jessica. "We've already promised her."

Mrs. Wakefield sighed. "I must say I'm relieved it wasn't the class money," she said. "I couldn't believe that you'd actually do something like that."

"Mother!" said Jessica. "How could you even *think* that?"

Mrs. Wakefield folded her arms. "That still

doesn't change the fact that you've taken money that isn't yours, young lady," she said.

"And I think you two girls owe some people apologies for the lies you told," Mrs. Riteman added. She frowned at Ellen. "Especially to your poor little brother."

Ellen grimaced. "But we were planning to tell the truth," she said. "That's why Jessica brought the chest back from her house today."

"That's still no excuse," said Mrs. Riteman. "Look at all the problems you made for yourselves by not being honest in the first place."

Ellen and Jessica squirmed. "I'm sorry," said Jessica.

"Me too," said Ellen.

Meanwhile, Laura had been busy reading the letters. Now she finished the last one and slipped it back into its envelope. Her eyes were misty. "Thank you, Grandmother Jane," she said quietly.

"What for?" interrupted Ellen.

Laura picked up the two portraits and gazed at them. "For helping me make the right decision," she said. She saw the girls' puzzled expressions and held up the portrait of the man. "This wasn't the man my grandmother married," she said.

"You mean she didn't choose William," said Ellen. "After all that?"

Laura shook her head sadly. "I loved my grandmother dearly," she said. "We were always very close. My grandfather was a nice man too. A successful lawyer. But there was always something missing between them." She paused long enough to look at the portrait of the man again. "Now I know why," she said softly. "My grandmother made the wrong choice. She let the one she really loved get away."

Laura picked up the letters once more and smiled. "But the story has a happy ending," she said. "Because right now I have to make a choice too. The same choice my grandmother had to make. To go with the man I love isn't going to be easy. My family's against him, my friends think I'm not being practical . . ." Her eyes misted over and again she looked at the girls. "But Grandmother Jane has helped me make up my mind," she said firmly. "If she were here right now, I know she'd approve of my decision."

For a moment no one said anything. Then Jessica sat down on the steps and hugged her knees. "How romantic," she said with a sigh.

"A perfect ending," Ellen said. She tried to imagine Laura's boyfriend. He was probably very handsome.

"I'd like you girls to keep the two hundred dollars," Laura added with a twinkle in her eye. "As reward money."

"Wow!" said Jessica. Things were beginning to work out even better than she'd expected.

"That's very generous of you, Laura," said Mrs. Riteman. "Are you sure?"

"Absolutely," she answered. "Consider it a gift from my grandmother."

Jessica and Ellen looked at each other and grinned.

Quietly, Mrs. Riteman turned to Ellen. "Wasn't Mark with you when you found that money?" she asked.

Ellen started to protest. "But—"

Mrs. Riteman gave her a stern look.

"OK," Ellen said reluctantly.

"Is there any money left?" said Mrs. Wakefield.

"I have about twenty-five dollars," Jessica admitted.

"Me too," said Ellen.

"Then I think that fifty dollars belongs to Mark, don't you?" said Mrs. Riteman.

It seemed like a small sacrifice to Jessica, considering the trouble they could have been in otherwise. "Fine by me," she said.

Ellen nodded her head in agreement. "It's OK with me too," she said.

At that moment Mark rode into the driveway on his bicycle.

"Perfect timing," Mrs. Riteman said to the girls. "Your first apology."

Mark's eyes popped out when he saw the treasure chest sitting on the front porch beside his mother. He threw his bike down on the lawn and hurried up the steps. "Mom, look!" he shouted, pointing.

Mrs. Riteman nodded. "Ellen and Jessica have something to say," she replied.

Ellen stared at the porch steps. "We're sorry we lied about finding the money," she said.

"We're going to give you fifty dollars," Jessica added. "Your share."

Mark threw his book bag in the air and let out a loud whoop. "Yippee!" he cried.

Ellen rolled her eyes. It was hard to give up that money, especially to Mark. But she and Jessica had learned an important lesson. She decided right then and there that no matter what, she'd never do anything dishonest again.

Ten

◇

Elizabeth and Amy raced up the Ritemans' driveway. "Mom, Mom," Elizabeth called. "Don't get mad at Jessica. It was all a big mistake. Amy and I found the class money."

"We're serious," said Amy, panting from running so fast. "Call Ms. Wyler if you want. We just gave it back to her."

"You what?" said Mrs. Riteman.

"We found the money in the supply closet," Amy repeated.

Jessica could hardly believe the news. "You see?" she said triumphantly. "It wasn't us. That proves it!"

Elizabeth rushed over to her sister. "Jess, I'm really sorry," she said. "I should never, ever have doubted your word. Will you forgive me?"

Jessica stared stubbornly at the ground. She'd really earned this apology, and she wanted to drag it out for as long as possible. "Maybe," she said in an offended voice.

"Please?" said Elizabeth.

"You hurt my feelings a lot," said Jessica. She

looked up and saw her mother watching her. "But I guess I can forgive you," she added hastily.

"And I'm sorry too," said Amy. "I spread the rumor about you and Ellen taking the money because I thought everyone was blaming me."

"We accept your apology," said Ellen.

Elizabeth looked around the porch and suddenly noticed the stranger.

"This is Laura," said Mrs. Wakefield. "Perhaps Jessica and Ellen should tell you the rest of the story."

As the two girls explained about the chest, Amy and Elizabeth listened in amazement. When they were finished, Jessica sat back. "I owe you and the class an apology for lying about where I got the Walkman."

"And the earrings," Ellen chimed in.

"Apology accepted," said Elizabeth with a grin. "I'm so glad we're all friends again and that everything has worked out. Let's never do that again. It was awful."

"I know," said Jessica.

Mrs. Wakefield put her arms around both her girls. "Thank goodness you two are speaking to each other again," she said. "The house was beginning to sound like a library."

Jessica laughed. "Oh, Mom, I thought you liked the peace and quiet."

"Not *that* much quiet," said Mrs. Wakefield.

That evening at dinner Mr. Wakefield and Steven listened as Jessica and Elizabeth told about the surprising events that had happened that day.

"Laura sounds like a lovely person," said Mr. Wakefield after they'd finished.

"She is," said Mrs. Wakefield. "In fact, we've invited her and the Ritemans to dinner tomorrow night."

"We have?" said Jessica and Elizabeth at once.

"You two were so busy making up, you missed the invitation," Mrs. Wakefield said, laughing.

"Can we barbecue out by the pool?" asked Jessica.

"I don't see why not," said Mrs. Wakefield.

Jessica grinned. Everything was working out perfectly. She glanced over at Elizabeth and noticed there was something still troubling her. Jessica knew at once what it was.

Later that evening Elizabeth heard a knock on her door. "Lizzie, it's me," said Jessica. "Open up."

Elizabeth came to the door.

"There's something I want to say," Jessica began. "It's about your speech."

Elizabeth's face fell. "Yes?"

"I just wish there were some way I could make it up to you," Jessica blurted. "I've been thinking. How about if I make an announcement over the loudspeaker about you?"

Elizabeth's eyes grew wide. "Jess! You can't do that! No one except Mr. Clark can use the loudspeaker."

"Well, what if I sneaked into the office, tied up Mr. Clark, and then grabbed the mike?" Jessica said, trying to sound as serious as possible.

Elizabeth clapped her hand over her mouth and

gasped. Then she realized that Jessica was only joking, and broke into a howl of laughter.

"T-t-tie Mr. Clark up?" Elizabeth gasped, holding her stomach. Every time she looked at Jessica she cracked up all over again. "You're too much, Jess," she said finally. "What a crazy sister."

"I was only trying to help," Jessica replied.

"Thanks, but no thanks," Elizabeth giggled. She leaned her head forward and grinned mischievously. "I'll tell you what you *can* do," she said.

"What?" said Jessica.

Elizabeth playfully hit Jessica over the head with her pillow. "You can find my green sweater that you borrowed two weeks ago and never returned." She laughed. "If I'm going to lose, I might as well lose looking good."

The next morning Amy waited anxiously outside school. As soon as she saw Ken, she hurried over. "Did you hear the news?" she said. "Elizabeth and I found the class money in the supply closet."

"You're kidding!" said Ken.

Amy nodded and continued walking with Ken. "It was all a big mistake," she said. "Ms. Wyler misplaced it. Jessica and Ellen had nothing to do with it."

"That's great," said Ken. "I guess that means we get to go to Disneyland."

Amy took a deep breath. "I'm sorry I've been such a bad friend," she said. "It isn't even worth it to tell you why I was acting this way. I just want to apologize."

Ken stopped. "Really?" he said.

"Really," Amy replied.

Ken picked up his pace. "Are you coming to the game this weekend?"

"The Boosters are cheering," said Amy.

"Maybe we can go out afterward for ice cream," said Ken.

Amy's eyes lit up. "OK," she said. She remembered something else. "Can I invite a friend?"

Ken's face fell. "Who?"

"Someone I haven't seen too much lately," Amy continued with a sly grin. "Her name is Elizabeth."

Ken looked relieved. "Sure," he said. "Sounds good to me."

The news about the class money spread quickly, and by noon everyone in the school knew it had been found.

Despite all the excitement, there was one thing that Elizabeth hadn't forgotten about: student council elections. She wished she'd done a better job with the speech. She'd practiced it enough times that she felt she should have known it by heart.

Just before lunch she went into the cafeteria by herself to cast her vote. As she crossed the empty room, she noticed all the colorful posters lining the walls. Maybe next year she'd try again, she thought.

Elizabeth carefully filled out her ballot, being sure to mark a heavy X next to her name. "When will we know the results?" she asked a girl who was watching the ballot box.

"Mr. Clark will announce it over the loudspeaker this afternoon," said the girl.

Elizabeth nodded and quietly walked away.

That afternoon Elizabeth had English class with Mr. Bowman. As she slid into her chair and prepared to take out her notebook, Julie approached, her face red. "You won't believe what happened," she said in a confidential voice.

"What?" said Elizabeth.

Julie bent down to whisper in Elizabeth's ear. "Peter asked me to go to the Dairi Burger with him on Saturday," she said.

The bell rang and Julie sat down in the seat next to Elizabeth. Elizabeth grinned at Julie, wishing there were some way she and Julie could finish their conversation, but Mr. Bowman was very strict about talking. She tore a corner off a piece of notebook paper, wrote *Congratulations* and drew a happy face inside the *O*. She passed the note to Julie.

Julie smiled. "Thanks," she mouthed back.

Elizabeth nodded and bent over her textbook.

Mr. Clark's announcement didn't come over the loudspeaker until nearly three o'clock. Everyone could hear him tapping on the microphone before he spoke. "Shirley, is this thing on?" he asked Mrs. Knight, the school secretary. Elizabeth giggled to herself as she imagined Jessica crashing through the door, taking over the office. There was some more background confusion, and then Mr. Clark said, "We're pleased to announce our new student council members." The class grew very quiet. "President, Olivia Davidson." There was loud applause. "Uh, boys and girls, if you're applauding, please hold it until the end. Vice President, Tom Sleeter. Secretary, Virginia Walker. Treasurer, Elizabeth Wakefield."

Elizabeth's mouth fell open. How could she possibly have won? It must be a mistake.

"On behalf of myself and all the teachers, I want to thank everyone who ran this year," Mr. Clark was saying. "You were all fine candidates, and we had some very close races."

Elizabeth looked around the room. People were smiling at her now and applauding. The bell rang, and everyone stood up.

"You won!" said Julie. "You must be so happy."

Elizabeth had a puzzled expression on her face. "But Peter's speech was so good," said Elizabeth. "Mine was awful."

"*I* voted for you," said Julie.

"You did?" said Elizabeth.

"I thought you were better qualified," Julie answered. "You told us that in your speech."

"But didn't you like Peter?" said Elizabeth.

Julie blushed. "Peter's speech was the funniest thing I'd ever heard," she said. "But you were the person who would do the best job."

Elizabeth nodded slowly. "I guess I see what you mean," she said.

Julie and Elizabeth made their way out into the hall. Julie squeezed Elizabeth's arm. "Look who's coming."

Peter approached Elizabeth and stuck out his hand. "Congratulations," he said.

"Thanks," said Elizabeth. Julie stood awkwardly at Elizabeth's side.

"Where are you going?" he inquired.

Julie looked at Elizabeth. "Uh, my house," said Julie quickly. "To celebrate. Want to come?"

"Sure," said Peter.

Amy came crashing down the hall. "Elizabeth!" she squealed. "You won!" When she saw Peter standing there, she stopped.

"It's OK," said Peter. "If my best friend won, I'd be happy too."

"You're right," said Amy. She slapped Elizabeth on the back. "All right, Elizabeth," she said.

"We're just going over to my house to celebrate," interrupted Julie. "Want to come?"

Amy grinned. "Sure," she said. "Your mom makes the best chocolate chip cookies in the world. Let's go." Laughing and joking, the four friends headed out the door.

Later that evening Jessica was busy helping Mrs. Wakefield set the table for their dinner guests. As she raced around the patio, she listened to Toy Car on her Walkman. "Be mine, be mine," she sang loudly as she tossed down the forks and spoons.

"Jessica, be careful!" shouted Mrs. Wakefield from the other room.

Jessica nodded and spun around. She had a good reason to be in such a great mood. Laura had called that afternoon to say that after she'd told her boyfriend her decision, he'd decided to drive down from his home in San Francisco to spend the weekend with her. He'd be joining them for dinner that evening. Jessica was ecstatic. She and Ellen had already spent about an hour on the phone discussing it.

Jessica looked up and saw Elizabeth standing nearby. "Did you hear the good news?" she shouted. "Casey is coming to dinner!"

Elizabeth looked puzzled.

"Laura's boyfriend," Jessica explained. "He was so excited when Laura told him she would marry him that he's driving down for the weekend. He said he wanted to be with her. Isn't that the most romantic thing you ever heard?"

Elizabeth smiled and held up a fork. She said something Jessica couldn't hear over the noise of her Walkman. "What?" said Jessica, pulling off the earphones.

"You put two forks at Casey's place," Elizabeth said. "He's going to have a tough time with his steak."

Jessica looked horrified. "Thank you so much, Lizzie," she said. "I would have been so embarrassed." The door bell rang and Jessica shrieked. "It's them! They're here!" She and Elizabeth both raced for the door and threw it open.

Their faces fell. "Oh, it's just Dad," said Jessica.

Mr. Wakefield laughed. "That bad, huh?" he asked.

"We were hoping it was Laura and her boyfriend," Elizabeth explained.

Mr. Wakefield nodded. "I'm glad to see you two getting along again."

Jessica's eyes lit up. "*Now* is it time for us to hear the secret you told us about?" she asked.

"Not quite yet," said Mr. Wakefield with a twinkle in his eye. "I'm still waiting for the right moment."

"But when is the right moment?" said Elizabeth. Now that she and Jessica were speaking again, even she was getting curious.

"You'll see," said Mr. Wakefield mysteriously.

The barbecue was a big success. As it turned out, Laura and Casey were the last guests to arrive.

When Jessica, Elizabeth, and Ellen opened the door, Jessica's heart stopped. Casey was about the handsomest man she'd ever seen. Tall, blond, and blue-eyed, he looked just like Parker Smith on *Love and Lace*, Jessica's favorite soap opera.

As Laura introduced him, he kept his arm around her waist.

"He's so cute, I'm about to die," Ellen whispered to Jessica.

Jessica stood transfixed as Laura finished her introductions.

"We're so happy you both could join us tonight," said Mrs. Wakefield.

Casey grinned. "I wanted to meet the people who were responsible for changing Laura's mind," he said.

"Don't thank us, thank Grandmother Jane," exclaimed Jessica. She was instantly embarrassed for blurting out like that, but Casey and Laura didn't seem to mind.

Laura held out her left hand. On her ring finger was a shiny new diamond. "Casey's been keeping this in his dresser drawer for months." She laughed. "I guess he couldn't wait for me to get back to San Francisco to put it on."

Casey squeezed Laura's hand. "I didn't want

you to change your mind, sweetheart," he joked.

"Why don't we all go out by the pool?" said Mrs. Wakefield, smiling. She turned to Casey. "I'm sure the girls would love to hear where you and Laura met."

Jessica cringed. Why did her mother have to ask such embarrassing questions?

"At the Laundromat," Casey replied with an easy grin. "I couldn't figure out how to work the machines."

"What an excuse!" Laura interrupted gleefully.

"Actually," Casey admitted, "I'd seen her around the neighborhood for months, but couldn't figure out how to manage an introduction. One day when I saw her heading for the Laundromat, I ran home, pulled the sheets off my bed, and hurried after her."

"Here was this guy standing around the washing machines with no soap and no change!" Laura said.

"So then you fell in love?" said Ellen.

Laura and Casey exchanged glances. "Sort of," said Laura. "I was dating someone else at the time. David. I'd been going out with him since high school. His parents and mine were best friends and they were really pushing for us to get married."

Casey took Laura's hand. "Laura was never really happy with the idea, but she didn't want to rock the boat."

"Until now," Laura added.

"We're so happy everything has worked out," said Mrs. Wakefield.

"And how," added Mark Riteman, no doubt thinking about the money he'd been given.

Mr. Wakefield put on a blue barbecue apron. "I don't know about anyone else, but I'm getting hungry for those steaks," he said. Everyone laughed. Mr. Wakefield handed Steven and Sam Riteman some long-handled forks. "How about some help, boys?" he said.

Over dinner, Steven, Sam, and Mark enjoyed hearing Casey's college football stories. Laura told everyone about her grandmother and talked about how there had once been a chicken coop in the Ritemans' backyard. Everyone had a wonderful time.

After the guests left, Jessica leaned against the front door and sighed. "I'll never forget this night as long as I live," she said. "Come on, Lizzie," she said, laughing. "Mom and Dad worked hard all night. Let's go load the dishwasher."

"Let me get this straight," said Steven. "You're actually volunteering?"

Jessica sniffed and stuck her nose in the air. "What's so strange about that?" she asked.

Elizabeth put her arm around Jessica. "Yeah, Steven," she said. "What's so strange about that?"

Mr. Wakefield picked up a sponge and threw it at Steven. "Come on, son," he said. "If the girls are doing the loading, you can wipe down the counters." He grinned at Elizabeth. "You can help the new student council member in the family."

"That's right," said Jessica. She spun around and pointed to Elizabeth. "That's my twin!" She turned to face her father. "*Now* can we hear your secret?" she asked.

Mr. Wakefield laughed. "What did I tell you?"

"You're waiting for the right moment," the girls said in unison.

Mr. Wakefield nodded. "Exactly," he said. "And this isn't it."

Jessica carefully rinsed off a dinner plate and handed it to Elizabeth. What in the world could the secret be? She peeked over at her father again, but he was already busy putting away the grill. Jessica handed the last dish to Elizabeth and dried her hands with a dish towel. Maybe her father would even tell them tonight, or tomorrow! Jessica gave an excited little skip across the room as she imagined the far-off exotic place where her father was bound to be taking them!

What is Mr. Wakefield's secret? Find out in Sweet Valley Twins 12, **KEEPING SECRETS.**

We hope you enjoyed reading this book. All the titles currently available in the Sweet Valley Twins series are listed at the front of the book. They are all available at your local bookshop or newsagent, though should you find any difficulty in obtaining the books you would like, you can order direct from the publisher, at the address below. Also, if you would like to know more about the series, or would simply like to tell us what you think of the series, write to:

Kim Prior,
Sweet Valley Twins,
Transworld Publishers Ltd.,
61–63 Uxbridge Road,
Ealing,
London W5 5SA.

To order books, please list the title(s) you would like, and send together with a cheque or postal order made payable to TRANSWORLD PUBLISHERS LTD. Please allow the cost of the book(s) plus postage and packing charges as follows:

All orders up to a total of £5.00   50p
All orders in excess of £5.00   Free

Please note that payment must be made in pounds sterling; other currencies are unacceptable.

(The above applies to readers in the UK and Republic of Ireland only)

If you live in Australia or New Zealand and would like more information about the series, please write to:

Sally Porter,
Sweet Valley Twins,
Transworld Publishers (Aust) Pty. Ltd,.
15–23 Helles Avenue,
Moorebank,
N.S.W. 2170,
AUSTRALIA

Kiri Martin
Sweet Valley Twins,
c/o Corgi and Bantam Books New Zealand,
Cnr. Moselle and Waipareira Avenues,
Henderson,
Auckland,
NEW ZEALAND